ROSEWALL

PAUL BILIC

ROSEWALL

A Meditation

TAMBURLAINE

2004

First published in 2004 by
Tamburlaine
13 Kilner House
Clayton Sreet
London SE11 5SE

ISBN 0-9541679-2-9

A CIP catalogue record for this book is available from
the British Library

Typeset in Garamond 12/13pt
from the author's disk by Scriptmate Editions

Manufacture coordinated in UK by Book-in-Hand Ltd
20 Shepherds Hill London N6 5AH

PART ONE

CONFUSION

ONE

Hare remembered the first time he met Lynch.

Remembering the hotel room he had stayed in, the slim bed with its crimson bedspread and bolster, and his way of sitting on the bed, his arms down by his sides, his hands pushing into the soft ridges and ruffles of the elaborately decorated counterpane. He sat like that with his head bowed when he was trying to decide what to do: sit on the bed or sit at the desk; stay in or go out; go out for a long time or go out for a short time. Or then he might lie down, placing his head down gently on the bolster. This was the way life had organised itself for short-arsed Hare.

He was living in one of those limbos life sometimes doles out for limited periods. He was waiting. A man was paying the hotel room for him.

The hotel was in a back street of the Opera House. It was a perfectly respectable hotel. How many stars was it now? Was it two or was it three? It was a district of slanting alleys and narrow streets shifting or sliding away at angles, obtuse and acute, as if a haphazard intelligence had positioned them that way. They were the arteries and capillaries of the Opera House: so, in a sense, part of a pre-meditated scheme; which was odd, because what kind of a scheme would it be? The passages were just shafts and fissures in a great block of masonry.

It was late October. There was frost. Winter already. In the passageways ice. At night the stillness hummed. Hare spent his time queuing up for tickets for the opera. There were all kinds of queues. It took weeks of discreet inquiries to get to know the ins and outs of all the opera queues. There was one particular queue that started early in the morning for the opening of the East Wing box-office at eight o'clock for all the tickets that had not been sold for the Italianate Amphitheatre going cheap for just a few miserable crowns. It was in this queue that Hare met Lynch.

It was a flat face, as though the frontal bones of the cranium, the mandible and the maxilla, the zygomatic and the frontal bone itself, were not the veritable shelter of the brain, but mere two dimensional facade like stage flats. Only the nose emerged from out the flat surface; though not long, it was so strikingly protuberant that it was as if stuck on.

As Hare rounded the side of the arcade that ran along the side of the opera building, he saw the figure of Lynch standing by the railings in the customary place where the queue began. The pavements were frosted over. Hare walked cautiously. Lynch must have heard him approaching. Hare took up his place behind the gaunt figure. It was a figure he recognised from previous queues.

—Good morning, he said.

—Yes, answered Lynch without turning.

—It's bitter, said Hare and stamped one foot.

Lynch grunted.

Hare waited for a moment. He could smell a kind of acidic perfume coming off the other man. He wondered whether it really was a perfume. It was more the coarse chemical odour of bunsen-burners and primitive gunpowder.

—I'm staying in the hotel out the back there, said Hare. When I can't get to sleep I come out here and do the mornings. It's handy in that way. The hotel, I mean. Otherwise, I don't suppose I'd have the courage to queue up.

Lynch turned his head slightly so that he was looking at the railings obliquely and perhaps caught Hare in the corner of his eye. His lower jaw seemed to slip from where it was slung up by the temporal bone at the base of the skull.

—And as for me, he said at length. I come here after an evening at the Opera Grill. Otherwise, I dare say I wouldn't bother either. As I don't live in the quarter.

—The Opera Grill, repeated Hare. I've seen that. Now where have I seen that? It's a neon sign somewhere. It runs vertically down the edge of a building. It's a green neon sign. That's it. It's on Pizzay Street, just at the back there. You know, that's only a stone's throw from my hotel. What a coincidence! How's the grub?

—There's no grub.

—It's a grill, isn't it?

—No.

—Oh. I would have thought it was a restaurant of some kind.

—No, no. It isn't a restaurant. It's more in the manner of a club.

It was at this juncture that the lean stranger changed the trajectory of the conversation and fell to interrogating Hare as to why he was staying in a hotel and why he didn't look for a flat in the area, as he had certainly been staying there for quite some time now because (if he didn't mind it being said) his was a face one couldn't help noticing these past weeks in the morning queue.

When Hare got back to the hotel, he noticed how they'd put the glass he'd appropriated as his vodka glass back to the much more practical use as a toothbrush holder.

In the evening in the opera itself Hare caught sight of Lynch in the company of a beautiful woman with blond hair. A real blond. Her hair went right down. It took Hare's breath away. He exchanged only a brief greeting, thinking that Lynch would perhaps prefer not to be approached. A blond like that, Hare thought, was quite a catch. Hare, as usual, was unescorting.

The next day Hare made it his business to go and have a look for the Opera Grill club. He went and stood on Pizzay Street and looked up at the neon sign which ran down from the fourth to the second floors along the angle of the building. The ground floor was a bar. Hare went in and asked where he might find the Opera Grill club. They told him the Opera Grill club was the name of a restaurant that had gone out of business donkey's years back and that the neon sign was all that remained. It was kept illuminated in the evening by the proprietor of the bar in the hope of drawing people into the recess of the street. Hare asked what there was on the second, third and fourth floors of the building. The proprietor of the bar was not too sure but thought they were lawyer's offices or insurance offices, one or the other.

Hare went out into the street again. It was odd. He looked up at the Opera Grill sign. It was as if the sign were the only thing that existed of this club. Could it be that Lynch had meant this little bar, whose name (now he came to look at it) was the Commedia bar and which closed every evening at nine o'clock on the dot, or so the owner had assured him. Surely not. In which case it must be behind or tucked within the building. Hare popped his head into the doorway. Then he stepped in a little way. He looked up the dark stairwell past the twists of the banister to a dirty pane of skylight six floors up. It was hardly possible to imagine Lynch escorting his beautiful blond catch up those dusty slab stairs. No. Inconceivable.

When Hare got back to the hotel he unwrapped the bar of soap they provided pristine every day. He washed his face long and hard until he smelt the soap on his skin. He looked at his flat fingernails. They were impeccable. The room was warm inside. He took his clothes off and lay down on the bed, placing his head down carefully on the bolster.

His dreams were not narratives. They were all part of one immense globe onto which details were grafted over the nights, details which might clarify or complicate the whole. The premature winter. The hum of the silence. Footsteps falling on the floor above. His memory of things, like the footfalls, soft, then not there anymore, like kisses. The smell of the soap. The feel of his own highly manicured hands. Lynch took up his place there; a highly developed primate with a mouth like a trap.

TWO

It was a few days later that the two of them met again. This time in the bar of the hotel foyer at the interval of one of the evening shows. Hare, in fact, was not attending the show but happened to be having a drink in the bar, waiting for the results from the bear-baiting to be flashed up on the bar terminal. It was strange that Lynch should be there as it was the same show as a few nights previously. He was accompanied by a woman again; this time, a redhead, shorter, with freckles.

Hare came up behind them and clapped Lynch on the back.

—Well, what's all this about? he said, affecting a bluffness hardly warranted from his cursory meeting with Lynch. This Opera Grill of yours. Where is it?

As Lynch turned towards Hare an expression of sadness seemed to darken his features. It might have been his attempt to contain any manifestation of surprise, but it presented itself to Hare as a sudden and unbearably profound melancholy which closed on his face like a shutter.

—This is Dittmar, said Lynch, presenting his lady friend.

—Charmed, said Hare, taking a look at her.

They talked for a minute. The Opera, the tickets, the weather. Dittmar was leafing through her programme.

—And what about the Opera Grill? asked Hare, remembering only when the alarm was ringing for the second half of the show.

—We're going there after the show. Want to join us? answered Lynch, adjusting a buckle on his leather jerkin.

—I'm curious to find out where it is at least.

—We'll see you in the foyer after the show.

—I can't imagine where it is. You know, I've had a little look for it myself. The sign I know very well, Hare went on, looking from one to the other. She was a looker, the redhead. How did he net them?

—Until then, was Lynch as he escorted her away.

It was streaming with rain when the three of them came out of the Opera house. They walked along under the arcade before crossing the road to the Commedia bar.

—Closed! said Hare, intrigued as to where Lynch would lead them. He asked the redhead if this was her first time in the Opera Grill. She said it wasn't. '*Absolutely not!*' was how she put it. She turned her bright eyes on him in earnest. The tart, he thought. There was a smudge of something on her cheekbone.

They went further down the road towards Little Pizzay Street and turned into an impasse on the left. They stopped outside a tobacco shop and Lynch fumbled for a key in the pocket of his opera coat.

Inside the tobacconist's it was completely dark. They all stood together in close confinement for a moment or two as if in a dark lift. Hare smelt the perfume of the redhead. Blackberry. Was that possible? It's a pipe shop, Lynch was saying. Dittmar let out a nervous laugh and Hare said it was ingenious.

In a moment Lynch had drawn back a curtain. A narrow trace of light under a door at the end of a corridor illuminated their way. They trailed down the corridor in single file. Lynch took out another key and led them into the next room.

—Cloakroom, he said, but before they'd had time to notice he'd opened up what seemed like a cupboard door and they were stepping up a wide staircase towards a yellow door through which they heard the voices of a great party. Lynch knocked and the door swung wide open to him. It was this, the Opera Grill.

Moreover, it was on this occasion, Hare's first visit to the Opera Grill, that the gaunt primate Lynch, seated at one end of the Long Table in the Smoker's Lounge surrounded by his associates and collaborators of whom the redhead Dittmar, the blond of the previous night, Gloucester (an Engineer as he termed himself though he was referred by the others as Gloucester the Executioner) and Warwick the Photographer, first exposed the terms of what he called his brush with the scoundrel Rosewall. Warwick the Photographer, an immensely tall man, craned forward and grinned to hear what must have been a familiar story.

It was in the following terms that Lynch first expressed it:

—Rosewall, he said, slicking the hair back over his cranium. Or a lion rampant with impaled wolf on a field of fleur de lys azure…

—Rosewall's coat-of-arms, whispered Warwick to Hare across the table.

—Or so we were led to believe, went on Lynch. It was only in my researches in the National Guild Library that it occurred to me one day that the impaled wolf did look rather like an impaled dog. I had a particular dog in mind. One that trails around the stockyards at night. A labrador. Is that the name?

Lynch looked across to Gloucester, who smiled and nodded back at him. Hare took a sip from his pot of beer.

—And it occurred to me what if it was an impaled labrador? What would that make of Rosewall's claim to legitimacy? An impaled labrador on a field of fleurs de lys azure or rather on a field of narcissi because when you examined the original seal closely you find that these are pretty odd fleurs de lys. I've never seen fleurs de lys like them and, god only knows, I've got enough of them in my back yard out in Tassin. So now we're getting down to it. An impaled dog in a field of buttercups. So I looked through the annals. Impaled labrador on field of buttercups but no lion rampant. No lion rampant. This stopped me in my tracks for a moment. But, lo and behold, Volume Sixteen of the Complete Heralds Almanac, no lion rampant but weasel rampant. Compare with the original seal and there's no doubt about it. It's no lion at all. No lion but a weasel!

The party roared with laughter. Hare smiled around him at the others.

Warwick the Photographer was slavering his appreciation of the story with little gasps from the back of his throat and scratching uncontrollably with his fingers on the tabletop. The blond had thrown her head back in mirth. Her mouth was open wide and Hare could make out the width of her band of teeth set in her mouth like a brace.

THREE

The day of the All Saints, the hotel was practically empty. The receptionist told them there were only four people in residence for the weekend. All Saints had fallen on a Friday. Hare had been out for a late breakfast of rolls and egg, coffee and vodka. He wandered back to the hotel filing his fingernails. It was cold, with sunshine.

When he got back to his room he drew the heavy curtains together to darken it. He went over to the sink. He took one of the clean white towels off the rail and laid it out on the floor. He took his trousers and socks off and sat on the towel. Then, lifting up his legs, he hooked his feet into the bidet and ran water, hot and cold together. That way he washed his feet and exercised his abdominals at the same time. It was a little hotel trick of his. After a few minutes he dried his feet on the towel he'd been sitting on. Waste not, want not. He put his trousers back on. He washed his face in warm water. He took a fresh towel and pressed it onto his face. He held it there. He breathed hotly into the shroud. The concave worm-ridden light was overlaid with worm-ridden dark. It suffused.

Rosewall. Hare went through it all again. Two years ago Rosewall's name had come to the fore. It had started when he presented a petition before the Council Chamber. A scroll of signatures. As impressive a list as you could wish to see. People started asking themselves the question. Who was he, this unknown who had been chosen or who had chosen himself to represent such a distinguished body? The popular press looked into the matter. It came out that he wasn't such an unknown after all. He had claims, this Rosewall. A lineage going right back and a rampant lion on the coat-of-arms, that is to say, one of the forty existing families with theoretical claims on the unoccupied throne of the land. This unknown was no nobody at all, and the popular press took him up as their champion. The petition was trivia. The Livestock Bill; calling for the halt to all traffic of livestock through the inner-city precincts. It wasn't the petition that struck the chord. It was the names on Rosewall's list. For a man's name is his most solemn possession, and men such as those who were on that list don't set their signatures down at the drop of a hat and for a nobody.

In fact, Hare saw it now that from the moment the news about Rosewall started sifting through, from the moment the press suddenly, seemingly randomly—though nothing was ever random—started taking an interest in this unknown, from the moment even he first heard the name, he had known, immediately seen, albeit unknowingly, albeit unseeing, that some huge creaking about-turn of the city was underway; and that his life, Hare's life, along with so many other lives, was bombed or undermined. As for Hare himself, his life had caved in. The whole construction that had weathered and could weather still the sternest of barrages had crumbled when he heard the name Rosewall. The first time he had heard the name it had crumbled. He saw it now and recognised that from the very start, if it had been a start, he had known, albeit unknowingly, that it had all caved in within him. The name had sufficed. The name Rosewall, first heard like that in streets or in bars or at corners, uttered or mumbled, Rosewall; then in sentences, whole ones, taking its place in the clause like a regular part of speech, a noun, proper, joined up to all the rest, verbs and the like, adjectives, prepositions, adverbs, conjunctions, or sometimes hid in the embrasure of a pronoun, peeping from out the nook, Rosewall; coming round and round again in all his guises, in stories or anecdotes or arguments, hooded, cloaked, masked, in false mustachios and joke nose; or else in ink. The fugue of Rosewall, returning and reappearing, thrusting itself into Hare's life, and darkening it, draining it, leaving him stranded, blinking in the dust, his shoes scuffed and his shirt untucked, Hare panting hard on the lonely freeway, whilst in the distance speeding away with all the abandon of a cartoon character was Rosewall, the man who went thataway.

Rosewall took control of the new National Agenda party, which had been formed from the fall-out of the other major parties. Its image was polished and well defined; its politics unclear. A group of twelve surrounded Rosewall. For the most part actors and celebrities, people with leverage on the people, able communicators. The National Agenda party was buoyed up by the chaos in the city. Terrorism was rife and the Council Chamber was unable to stay the veering vessel under its command. And all this meant that when the elections came around the National Agenda party swept to power. Rosewall was made Public Protector for the three-year span laid down by the Constitution. In a period of fifteen months Rosewall had risen from being an unknown to the position of the most powerful individual in the land.

What had happened since Roswall's instatement as Public Protector—in the last seven months—had already sunk so deep into the lives of people as to exist already as a myth, something which had always been; so fearful were the events which had succeeded his taking of power.

The National Agenda party proceeded to a series of purges on foreigners. The popular press backed them up in this, denouncing all dissenting voices as traitors. A new constitution was drawn up, based principally on the Ur-charter of two centuries hence, which, amongst other things, increased the power of the Public Protector, especially if his name counted amongst one of the forty families having direct claims to the vacant throne. It was seen as an inevitability that sooner or later Rosewall, supported as he now was by the army, would reinstate the monarchy, and take up his claim to the throne. It was at this point that different factions began to panic. The Ur-charter constitution, which had been put through quietly and with a minimum of fuss, gave Rosewall complete protection. The only actions that could be taken against him were illegal. The acts of terrorism increased dramatically perpetrated by a body that was referred to as the Phalange by the popular press. Hardly a day went by without some new atrocity. The city was in uproar. And it was at this time, some thirty days ago, that Rosewall had disappeared.

Rumours abounded. He had fled after yet another assassination attempt. He had lost his nerve and got out while the going was good. Or else he was merely absent for a few weeks. A sabbatical of sorts. To gauge the state of the nation and commence the new Doomsday Book he had, according to the popular press, always dreamt of compiling. He had reinvested power in the Council Chamber—his Council Chamber—and was visiting his provinces disguised as a wandering abbot. Or else there was another version which had appeared in certain secret leaflets which had been distributed about the city. He had been made to stand down and tortured into submission on the pulley, that graphic and highly imaginative instrument of modern chamber warfare.

Who could tell where the truth lay? Certainly not Hare, a minor functionary of Wyvern, the all-powerful media agency, comprising television stations, radio outlets and popular press issues, a journalist of sorts, although a minor one, classed Gamma Triple Minus on the scale, with no more than a priority C pass-card. He breathed hotly into the towel. He imagined that his face had been annulled, that a great cliff had snatched him into it, had incorporated his outline into its stone. For a moment he almost wished it, for the earth to gape and harbour him.

He took the towel off his face and repursued his hotel existence. He liked to sit on the bed with important objects about him: his wallet with money in it; some food near him; a loved object; a future activity (a book to read or music to listen to). This all reassured him. The elements of his life were with him: security, comfort, love, a future. He sat at the table to write in his journal. In the semi-obscurity he could just about see to write, but was unsure whether his handwriting followed the lines on the page or diverged above or below the thin blue threads.

A knock came on the door.

Hare, though shocked, did not hesitate to open it.

—What do you want? he asked the man, who was looking straight past Hare into the room as if something were being hidden in there.

—I'm from the floor below, answered the man. We're not too many in the hotel today.

—Top marks for that one, snapped Hare, not without irony. It means we can get a bit of peace for once in a while, which I (for one) appreciate, so if you'll kindly excuse me, I'll ask you to go about your business and take your hand away from there, otherwise it's liable to get trapped when I shut the door in just one second.

—But this room's exactly the same shape as mine, said the man, striding in.

—Of course it is, said Hare. All the rooms are the same. The single rooms, I mean, of course.

He had remained standing at the door, but now turned on his heels to address the stranger who was over at the window.

—The view's different, mind. You can see the river. I can't. I look out the back to the courtyard.

—I'm very sorry for that, sir.

—Oh no. I dare say you get the noise of the street.

Hare moved swiftly across the room to his writing desk and closed the secret leaves of his journal before the intruder's eyes could get accustomed to the darkness and stray.

—That's why you draw the curtains, isn't it? To muffle the noise.

—It could be a reason.

—You see. I'm a bit of a detective.

—A bit of a housebreaker too.

—I'm no housebreaker, said the stranger.

—Well, I never invited you in.

—Excuse me one moment, said the man, drawing a large rag from his pocket on which he commenced blowing his nose, making a fierce, untextured sound, a blare such as comes from a hooter.

—Today, he said, as he was dabbing his nose with the rag and stuffing it back into his trouser pocket. Today is All Saints' Day. You'd be familiar with that of course. And, it being a holiday, people go off for a weekend...

—If you've come collecting for money, you'll get none from me. These are troubled times for us all, mister.

—I'm not collecting for money. I was just saying that people go off for the weekend. To get away from the city life, isn't it? That, I can understand. I can't go myself. I've got business to accomplish in the city... And yourself?

—I don't like leaving the city, answered Hare, who had poured himself water from the tap and was steadily sipping it.

—Is that so strange to you? he went on bitterly.

—Not so very strange.

—No. I don't ever leave the city. Don't ever leave the quarter for that matter. I like to be on my own territory.

He was standing at the sink with one hand grasping the cold-water tap. He was standing on one leg, casually.

—So, this is your territory, is it?

—This is where I am.

—I see what you mean.

He had taken his rag out again and was waving it around. Hare wished he wouldn't. Then, the visitor laughed for a moment.

—Well, put it this way, he began.

—Don't put it any way, said Hare. If you must know, I'm actually waiting for a young lady and I'd be best pleased if you let me wait in peace.

Hare was lying. There was no woman.

—I quite understand. The waiting is surely the most exquisite of all the pleasures associated with courting. No, what I wanted to say was this: today's the All Saints'. That's true…

—Oh, don't start all that again!

—But yesterday, if you'll just hear me out, yesterday was the All Souls'. Let's not forget that. And if that's the case, then let me put it this way. Yesterday was All Souls' and I'm here to make atonement as all good believers used to do on that particular day.

—Well and good. Now you've done it. Now get out!

—Atonement, he was saying again and waiting.

—What atonement? shouted Hare.

—Atonement. On the day when we are called to remember those souls that suffer for their sins…

—What are you talking about?

—...that live in a state of temporary suffering, I would recall to you your own conscience, sir.

—As regards whom, may I ask?

—Me, for example.

—You! In what way might my conscience be troubled by your presence?

—Atonement, Mr Hare.

—How do you know my name?

—I asked the hotel receptionist. A simple enough venture. Wholly without mystery, Mr Hare.

—Stop using my name like that.

—Like what?

—At the end of every sentence you speak.

—That's the first time I've heard of a man afraid of his own name.

—Would you like me to call the hotel manager, who happens to be a personal friend of mine.

—There's no need for that.

—What's your name anyway?

—Ah! Now he wants to know my name.

—You know who I am. Give me one good reason why I shouldn't know who you are.

—Now he changes his tune.

—Come on.

—Now he blows another tune.

—So what is it?

—Hold your horses, Mr Hare. I'll tell you. Only no flinching.

—What's he talking about?

—The name's Prospect. No flinching. Did I see you flinch? Prospect's the name.

—Good. Now get out.

—Of course. If you're waiting for a young lady, I quite understand your impatience. But let's entertain the possibility of a meeting in the not-too-distant future. For a little drink, you know. Why ever not? It gets the circulation moving. Gets a man on his toes. And besides, I'm not adverse. I told you that already, didn't I? I'm free this evening.

—I'm not.

—Still, soon, I think. Now that the ice is broken between us, we may as well make the most of it.

Before he left, he wiped his nose with the handkerchief, and then, using the same rag, mopped his brow. Hare closed the door softly behind him. He breathed deeply, taking care to inflate and deflate the stomach, as he knew was good for him. Under his arms he was sweating.

He went to the bed to lie down, tipping his head gently back until it was supported by the bolster.

Life was moving at the speed of light. It was fast arriving at that point when the plughole starts to loom large, when the scurf and grit and flakes of life and hopes take to spinning. In the stillness of the hotel bedroom he knew that light-rays were shuttling to and fro, and that thought, or sparks of thoughts, were leaping silently across chasms in his mind, and that, therefore, despite the apparent calm of this hotel bedroom, he was nevertheless being shunted along tracks of some description. From within, his organs, lungs, heart, kidneys, pancreas—all of which were gently caving in—as well as from without, history was accomplishing its business on him. And yet, for all this knowledge, he retained the sense that what counted might still be what resided in the stillness, in these moments that had been, so to speak (he knew it was only so to speak), rescued from history.

For the moment the street outside was calm. Maybe the Phalange took the All Saints' off too. Recently, the bombings had increased. People's behaviour was changing. They panicked or (worse still) started speaking to each other (strangers) in trams or trolleybuses or when they saw parcels somewhere without owners.

At any moment you might expect a flash of blinding light to step out to meet you, and if it was raining and you were wet and tired you might welcome it, in the one split instant when it came for you, opening your arms to it wide to embrace it, that sharp killing, letting it invade you, splatter you, teeth and face and bones into oblivion, because in one split instant it would all be over. Over. A last breath truly drawn. In and out and in sulphur finished.

FOUR

When the knock came on the door again he got up quickly
to open it. He was resigned.

—You know who I am, said Prospect.

He stepped into the room and sat down at Hare's desk.
He let his hands dangle down between his legs as though
to support the fall of his genitalia. They were dirty-nailed
hands, Hare noticed.

—You're from Wyvern, you're from the Agency, said
Hare.

—Got it in one, said Prospect.

Prospect breathed out and smiled.

—And now the question is. What are you up to? By
which I mean to say, it's a question Wyvern might well ask
of you, if it felt so inclined. Because, let's face it, after all,
here you are running up a fine hotel bill. And if you think
Wyvern is going to fork out, you might be very much
mistaken, Mr Hare.

Hare shifted the sole of his foot on the carpet and
scratched a hirsute region of his body.

—I don't know, he mumbled. The smack's gone out of
it.

Prospect slid a stare obliquely across over the stub of
his nose.

—You don't think of informing the Agency, I suppose, when the sap runs out of it, retorted Prospect.

—The smack, said Hare

—No, said Prospect. You don't think anything of the sort. You just stick around the hotel, drinking hotel vodka, using precious Wyvern funds.

—That's not true. I buy the vodka from my own pocket. Look! That's why I use the toothbrush holder as my vodka glass. And it's got me into trouble with the hotel management. It's drawn attention to me, made my position ambiguous. He's always plonking the toothbrush back in. The manager or one of his flunkies.

—As if you needed that to make your position ambiguous. Well, make no mistake about it, Wyvern's stopped forking out for the hotel. It's been paying through the nose long enough. Let me acquaint you with the facts. Let me re-acquaint you with the facts.

Prospect took a sheet of paper from his inside jacket-pocket.

He read: Hare. Age: Thirty-three. Height: 1 metre, seventy-two…

—Seventy-three, interposed Hare.

—I'll skip the rest of the physical characteristics and get straight to the point. Assignments: Opera House Duty. Concerts in Minor Rooms. Chamber Music and Lieder. Chocolate and Biscuit Manufactory Reports. Clocks and Watch-making etc etc. Stamps and Coinage. Heraldry and blasons.

Prospect looked up from the sheet and raised an eyebrow.

—The last article dates from six weeks ago. Your contract says one article a week plus news items three per week on average over a three-month period with one week off for research purposes. Need I go on?

—What's the Agency going to do?

—The Agency's one step from washing its hands of you, Hare, Prospect answered with lustre in his eyes.

Which meant that Hare would have to foot the hotel bill, or else creep out in the middle of the night, running the gauntlet of the all-night receptionist, a youngish man, with strong haunches. A youngish man, and now to boot, because of the toothbrush-holder, clearly on the qui-vive.

—Try and see this from the Agency's point of view, went on Prospect. There's no news from you for weeks. Not a word about the Rosewall coat-of-arms. You spend precious Agency funds on hotel vodka...

—I told you about the toothbrush holder.

—And when I ask you politely, ever so politely, as if it were Wyvern which had wronged you and not vice versa, when I ask you what's up, what do you tell me? The sap's gone out of it. You see my point of view? Are you understanding me loud and clear now? Are the cauliflowers out of those ears now? It's time for some straight questions and answers. Why's this sap gone out of it?

Hare reflected a moment.

—Rosewall, he said. It was the first time it had occurred to him.

Prospect was already not listening.

—Where is Rosewall? repeated Hare after a moment.

Prospect caught the end of the question.

—Exactly. And where are those coat-of-arms revelations we've been waiting for for weeks?

Hare had no answer.

Prospect smiled lasciviously.

—You haven't seen the new Wyvern manifesto, have you? You're not aware of recent changes. I'm sure some of those changes might interest you.

A pang of nostalgia went through Hare. He looked out into the street where snowflakes were slipping gently past the windowpanes. The winter feasts were coming fast. How was he to spend them? There was to be the traditional gathering of Wyvern functionaries. The Agency which had welcomed him to its bosom for the last three years. Wyvern had been like a mother to him; that was true enough. And how he had laboured to get the gamma triple minus priority. Now he was throwing it all down the laundry chute. Hare saw how it looked now. It was to be Hare alone, scarpering from his hotel, his old square suitcase flapping open as the all-night receptionist, the youngish man, hounded him, easily picking up on the scent, yea the trail of unwashed socks and underwear that the unwitting Hare strewed behind him. That was about the size of it. Meanwhile Wyvern would be indoors sipping its fancy cocktails. The Agency, each and every parcel of it, the cheapskate Prospect included, his little wedge nose in the cocktail glass, his dirty dog-hands clenching it, whilst Hare, in some minor footnote to the scene, fleeing, the youngish man panting hard on his heels, licking his youngish chops with a foretaste of the blood.

—You can be certain of one thing, said Prospect. I shall recommend to the Agency that the sternest of disciplinary actions be taken against you. That's right: gulp. Gulp, young man. Gulp, because if you thought of bowing out like a gentleman without giving a by-your-leave, then think again. I told you. Wyvern doesn't like being ditched; Wyvern will be taking steps.

Hare imagined Wyvern, which in heraldry meant two-legged dragon, taking its steps. And if it came to a scrap between the polyparcellular, polyvalent, polyjambist Wyvern and the monolithic metal Colossus of Rosewall, who would prevail? How would such a combat turn out? Wyvern turning tail and seeking shelter in the crevice; or, alternately, the great tin-man making himself scarce and clanking away over the Croix Rousse hill.

When Prospect had gone, Hare picked up the phone and asked for a bottle of hotel vodka from the receptionist. It was delivered up on a silver platter with a bucket of ice and a nice heavy glass.

—Just the very thing, said Hare, half to himself and half to the receptionist who was backing out of the room with a smug smile on his youngish face, happy that they had at last succeeded in luring Hare onto hotel vodka. Hare took his socks off. He sat upon the bed. The ice in the glass. The vodka onto the ice. Smelling it now. Watching the stirring of the colourless liquid on the rocks. Bringing it up to the lips. Tipping it. Drinking the vodka.

Alone, Hare contemplated his case. It was like turning out the contents of his trouser pockets and coming up with so many scraps of paper, old restaurant cards, toffee wrappers, farthing coins and stuff of forgotten ventures. It was meaningless. And all the meaninglessness managed to obscure his arch act, which was his desertion of Wyvern.

There was no making sense of it. He had spent years hoisting his career to where it was now. Only to let it all tumble in a few weeks of inactivity.

What had happened to him? In his own mind, it had started as a retreat. But he had retreated far, too far into himself. And now it was impossible to extract himself from the iron grip. Depending on how he wanted to gel his world, he might see it as newfound faith or newfound despair.

If it was faith, then faith in what? In himself? If that were the case, it would be easy to fix a word to his condition, a classic case, and the word direct from the first catechism. Pride.

Hare was proud. He was even vain, although (being by common consent a short-arse) he didn't have much to be vain about. And he was self-righteous. He always had to be right. He always had to have the last word. And then he was lazy. He felt he had the right to do nothing. Look at him now. Sitting on his bed in the hotel room. Slurping vodka down. Allowing himself thoughts, meditations. No man has the right to do nothing. This was Hare's first mistake.

FIVE

The photographer Warwick craned forward his long neck and poked his index finger out towards where Hare was filing his thumbnail.

—What's that? he said.

—A manicure, said Hare.

It was on the occasion of Hare's second visit to the Opera Grill Club. He replaced the nail-file in his wallet.

—Anything else in that vanity-case of yours? asked the photographer.

—Banknotes mostly, came Hare, in a spirit of fun and games leafing smartly through the wad (all the money he had or was likely to get now that he'd affronted Wyvern) no more than an inch from the photographer's nose.

—Impressive, said the photographer and leaned back in his wooden chair. It creaked under his undexterous shifting. He looked away.

Hare stowed the wallet safely back into his jacket pocket, then looked up, his face lighting up as though to enjoy the murkiness of the room.

—Anyway, started up the photographer. It seems a standard's been raised a few miles out. This'll be where they come to seize power. That stands to reason.

—Oh? Who told you that?

—A little bird told me so.

—And what else did this little bird say?

—Just that. That they've raised their banner in the field.

—And who's to say it means any more than it did last time? Just a lot of bravado. That's all it ever amounts to.

—Except that this time they're saying Rosewall's with them.

—Fiddlesticks!

—If you like.

—Fiddlesticks! Rosewall indeed!

Hare looked down to the zipper on his trousers. What if it were true? How would all this turn out then, the cold, his treks in the city, the nights, the stillness, the mineral world, his fortitude or lack of it?

—What if Rosewall were with them anyway? he said, looking up from his zipper though averting his gaze from the photographer.

Hare could see the figure of Lynch over at the bar. Not the entire skeleton, just the top half and front section, as if it were a bust fitted into a recess in the wall. Lynch's eyes were invisible, enmeshed in the shadowy texture of the long head, showing only as whirls of thinner oil paint, as if they had been plucked from their orbits and all that remained was a blood-boltered absence. The nose was a slim splinter, like a clinically fabricated partition of the left from right that cleft the rough oval in two.

The photographer was leaning across the table.

—It's only a rumour about Rosewall. You know what rumours are like, he said, watching Hare's eyes as they flickered back to their interlocutor. I'm trying to work you out, he went on. Do you know Dittmar?

—The redhead?

—That's the one. Do you know what I reckon?

—No.

—I reckon she's got her eye on you. In the conventional sense.

—What do you mean?

—Well, she said to me you were all right. Very nice, was what she said.

—That doesn't mean anything. People are often nice. Nice or not nice. It's got to be one or the other. If I'm nice it doesn't mean for one second she's got her eye on me. Some people think everybody's nice. That doesn't mean they've got their eye on everybody.

Warwick the Photographer laughed aloud and rapped fiercely with his knuckles on the table.

—What do you mean got her eye on me? asked Hare, not wanting to change the subject.

—The conventional sense, I told you.

Hare fingered his own ear.

—Of course, it may well be that she has, as you say, got her eye on me, but until such time as she summons up the courage to come and let me in on the secret I prefer to act as if I hadn't heard a thing.

—You know my name, don't you, said the Photographer. I'm Warwick.

He stood up and shook Hare's hand over the table.

—Hare, isn't it? Pleased to meet you, Hare. I'm a photographer, as you perhaps recall, which is why I think I might have an eye for this kind of business. Sometimes I photograph Dittmar. She models for the agency once in a while. Lynch's agency.

—What agency's that?

—Lynch has got this fashion agency. That's how I got to know him. Suitable Modes it's called. Ever heard of it?

—No. Anyway, the redhead doesn't look like a model. She's too short.

Hare withdrew his hand from the table and put it on his lap under the table.

—Needless to say, said Warwick. She's not really a model. She doesn't have the looks or anything.

—Course not.

—But she models for one particular image where Lynch finds her suitable. She was helping me put up curtains when she told me what she thought about you.

—What did she say then? queried Hare, keeping that little smile off his face because he knew she was one hell of a looker.

—I've told you.

Warwick jabbed over the table with his index finger again.

—Let me tell you what, he said. I'll tell her there's a job of work that needs doing. I'll arrange to meet her. We'll do a work session. I haven't told you about them, but she strips off, more or less, give or take a stitch. Last time she was in red socks and red pullover, just that. We'll do a few minutes, then I'll slip out on some pretext. That's where you come in.

—What are you talking about *that's where I come in*! said Hare hoarsely.

—Or, if you prefer, you can watch from behind the curtains, suggested the photographer.

—What do you mean? That's disgusting! muttered Hare, flushing.

—She's the one who's interested in you.

—I still don't know what you're talking about.

—I'm sure you can use your imagination.

—Stop that smirking, said Hare, raising his voice somewhat. What does she do exactly then?

—She helps me get the decor ready, answered Warwick, turning serious, his brows knitting. It's based on some painter Lynch is keen on. We have heavy red curtains, old heavy furniture, big windows but not much light. Then she strips off. I try and catch the dust in the room. You know the effect: half-light, dust, heavy furniture. He chooses her because she looks like one of the sluts in this guy's pictures. We follow the paintings as closely as we can. Of course, it's impossible to get so close. The medium doesn't allow it. Paint and film. Different material, all that.

—So why do you think she's keen on me then?

—I told you. She said she thought you were all right.

—All right. What does she mean *all right*? All right all right or a bit of all right? It proves nothing.

—Nothing proves nothing, does it? Look at Rosewall. There's no proof of that either, and then one day it turns out true. By the way, were you in the city when Rosewall came to power?

—That's a funny question.

—Why?

—Wanting to know a thing like that. No. I wasn't, if you must know. I was elsewhere actually. Rosewall was the last thing on my mind at the time I can tell you, he explained, looking at Warwick fiercely in the general region of his left eye. Owning up to working for Wyvern could be dangerous. The Agency was hated by many.

—Mind, he went on after a moment, when the silence had not caved in. My brother was here. Yes, my brother. He had business in the city. Yes, he was here all right.

—And where is he now?

—Good question, answered Hare and opened his mouth ostentatiously to frame an answer.

Suddenly Lynch was standing by the table.

—I was telling him about Vernon, said the lank photographer, shifting his chair across to make room for Lynch, who took his place next to them. The painter, added Warwick and looked over to Hare as though to prompt him.

Hare was watching Lynch. He could see the delicate grain of the dry skin on his forehead. A silence swelled.

—I've got this terrible blister on my heel, Lynch, said Warwick.

Lynch ignored him. He just stirred his head slightly on the axes of the shoulder pillory. Warwick fell silent and settled his large dinosaur body back in the wooden chair. Lynch addressed Hare.

—Tell me, why are you in the city?

—He's looking for his brother, piped up Warwick.

—You're looking for your brother, are you? took up Lynch without acknowledging Warwick's remark. And whatever makes you think he's in the city?

—He was here.

—But people are moving in and out of here all the time, said Lynch. Since the time of old Rosewall it hasn't stopped. Moving in and out. People with their furniture, their mattresses. Was he not one of those men, your brother? A man with a mattress. You're one of those men yourself, aren't you?

Hare shrugged himself a little and started looking for an answer.

—And by the way, went on Lynch. Didn't I tell you I have a little house out of the city just near the steeple Rosewall swung from. You know, the church tower he hid in during the battle of Tassin. He hid in there, then climbed up the steeple to get to the bell-tower. Imagine it! Swinging from the steeple top like a crazy old clown, shitting himself, chalk white with fear like an old Pierrot.

Warwick laughed loudly, knocking the table heavily with his red knuckles.

—That's strange, said Hare. I'd heard another story. I'd heard he climbed up the bell-tower to get a better view of what was going on through his binoculars.

—Don't believe everything you read. And mine makes for a better story, said Lynch. The point being that your brother no doubt got mixed up one way or other in the business, as one way or another we all did, and moved out somewhere else. Did you get in one way or another mixed up in the business?

Hare told him that he hadn't been there during the business and Lynch, laughing, asked him how he could know about the steeple story then. Hare said he'd heard it. Lynch asked if he'd heard it from his brother and Hare said no but from other men, strangers, the kind of men who were moving in and out with mattresses.

Then, in the silence, Warwick, after some scuffling with his finger-ends on the table to ignite the possibility of them listening to him, said: You should see the vanity-case he's got. Nail-filing. Manicuring set. The lot.

—Rosewall was a vain man also, took up Lynch.

—Did you ever meet him? asked Hare, leaning back in his chair to feign disinterest.

—Once I met him. Didn't meet him quite. Saw him at close hand. But you saw it from his bearing he was a vain man. It was a way he had of walking. He strutted. It was a way he had of taking little steps, as if restraining himself from trotting off downhill, aborted steps so to speak. But it looked arrogant. Of course, needless to say, we were sworn enemies. By which I mean to say, I was his sworn enemy. He wouldn't have known me particularly. I was just one of those trying to foil him.

—One of the leaders, said Warwick, leaning forward into Hare's line of vision. Lynch was one of the chiefs of the Anti-Rosewall movement.

—What Warwick means to say, said Lynch, is that I was one of the team that helped to find the legal loophole in his position, which, had he not fled of his own accord, would have led to his being incarcerated.

—Originally the Opera Grill Club! What was it? An anti-Rosewall club, announced Warwick, grinning from ear to ear. A secret club for a pocketful of men who were preparing to bring Rosewall crashing down.

—It's fairly secret now, said Hare.

—It's kept its Restoration character, said Lynch, looking round. Warwick looked round too, as though to shadow him.

—Until finally, restarted Lynch when he had focused on an anonymous group at the bar, we cleared him out and finished him off.

—I was saying, said Warwick. I was saying that there's rumours that they've hoisted their banner in the field again. And this time Rosewall's with them.

—There is no more Rosewall, answered Lynch dully.

—They're the rumours.

—I said it was fiddlesticks, said Hare.

—It's vulgar chit-chat, said Lynch.

—It's rumours, said Warwick, cowering a little. You know what rumours are.

Lynch slicked his black hair back over his cranium, then looked sharply away as if picking up a shard of conversation from somewhere else in the smoke-filled room. Or it might have been that the conversation had reached its necessary point of termination.

Later that night, sitting down at his hotel desk with a gulp of vodka, Hare thought about the redhead. She had her eye on him. The neutrality of her face for him. The freckles so pale they are hardly there. The whiteness of her face for him. The shocking, untouchable pallor. The nose almost erased away. The reddish hues of the hair, and the eyes, and the pale pink lips fringing or intermittently colouring it with the vividest of reliefs, in the way an illuminator fringes his sacred texts.

The winter cold. Hare laying his head on the bolster now. The work of the illuminators.

PART TWO

IMPOSSIBILITY

Lynch. Beginning with a vignette. Lynch smelling of soap, sitting very straight in his hard-backed chair and offering the side of his face for observation. He draws on a cigarette. The cigarette comes to red.

The first time Hare came back with him to the house near the steeple where, it was said, Rosewall hid or else observed the state of the battle of Tassin, Lynch explained he was waiting for an article of furniture for putting books on. The books were in piles on the brown carpet. It was mid-afternoon. Sunlight was making its way into the main room of the small house, slipping in through the small windows and laying itself out in parallelograms on the chocolate carpet and over the covers of the paperbacks. Further back, away from the window, drying sheets were slung across chairbacks like hammocks, blue-white like in adverts and creased. The scent of the soap powder hung in the air. There was a rug, all rolled up and leaning against the wall as if impatient to be moving in or out.

He offered Hare a drink and Hare opted for the vodka. Lynch found the bottle in the kitchen where it was rubbing shoulders with the bleach and the shoe brush. He poured it into the vodka glass and passed Hare a tin of

golden syrup with an old teaspoon stuck in it like the
sword in the stone. Hare, unsure whether this accompani-
ment was a tradition of some sort, limited himself to
putting his little finger in the tin and sucking at that.
Lynch drank milk.

When a phone rang Lynch picked it up and carried it
away to the other side of the room, and Hare could see
then, looking at the pads beneath the eyes (the soft area
above Lynch's cheekbone and below his eyelid) the fili-
gree capillaries which disappear and reappear in different
temperatures. Hare lowered his eyes. He knew why he had
been brought here. It was so they might go ever deeper
into the subject of Rosewall; that they might scourge him
or crown him. And for Hare too, these were Stations of
the Cross, stations on the winding path to some kind of
resolution. On the carpet the books, the sunshine, a
hammer, an empty yoghurt carton, an empty vase on its
side, a strapless blinking electronic watch.

Hare asked about the painter Vernon. Lynch strode
over to the other side of the room to produce a book.
Hare sat back on his chair and hunched his shoulders.
Lynch opened the book on Hare's knee. As he leaned over
to show him the picture Hare smelt the soap on his hands
and face.

It was the picture of a girl sitting in an armchair wearing red socks pulled up to just below her large flat
kneecaps and a red turtle-neck sweater. Red knickers. She
was reading a long narrow book with a pale green dust-
sheet. The floor was carpetless. One foot was on the
cushion of the chair; the other down on the ground, the
sole of the foot planted squarely on the stone slabs.

Lynch, still leaning over and somehow round him, was
speaking. Not daring to look up from the picture where
Lynch had imprisoned him, Hare tried to imagine the
long overshadowing oblong of Lynch's body, like a box
kite caught in momentary twisted repose in high sky.

—You have the cold from the slabs and the hot from the woman, he was saying. Their coexistence. There is no warm in the painting. No tepid. There is the respect of the cold for the hot and the hot for the cold. There is no invasion. Simple maintenance of the balance between the two.

Hare glanced up to Lynch's unbatting lids, behind which would be the dark box-room where Lynch filed his information away and in whose musty cupboard the raw, jelly, insecticide truth would be. He looked back down.

He imagined the redhead in the posture of the girl. He hunched up and scratched a place on his knee, where by rough magic an itch had come. Why had he agreed to follow Lynch out to the suburbs of this city, where as a general law he never went, to this house, a poor two-storey, three-roomed affair? There to crunch over sun-drenched but frosted grass, to come into a sitting-room in mid-afternoon and sit on a sitting room chair, taking his place with the drying sheets while Lynch produced some picture he was keen on, and then to find himself impris-oned by this picture of some anonymous tart with not a stitch to spare her blushes save what was red for danger, and Lynch above and around him like some ancient and jealous demi-god, casting his design with imperfect web. There to wait at the table fingering his vodka glass and to feel the stillness of the country all about him, because it was the country more or less, something he wasn't in the habit of enduring. Its great chasm was apt to knock the very breath out of him.

But he'd done it. He'd sat in the chair and said he'd take the vodka, so marking with a solemn shot (45% proof) this new space and unknown, unplanned future hour or two which he, in the grip now of superior forces—Lynch, the suburbs—could only bow to.

—The painter Vernon, said Lynch, still at that angle of his, his breath so close, never divulged a thing about his own life. His paintings were confidential articles. They are dispersed in private collections, rarely shown. He resisted the temptation to purposefully confuse the social sphere and the intimate domain where creation takes place. That, I might add by the by, is the game of some many of our artists these days. He was resolved in his discretion, haughty in his convictions. He was careful about his environment for his painting was tributary. His various lodgings reveal his nature: a love of pure layout, a lack of ornamentation, severe, a domain which best retains the imprint of past generations. Few knew of his whereabouts. He invited only those he could use, those he could portray. He lived in Lampshade Street in the second court that looks onto Thrush Street. There is a painting of that period that depicts the window looking onto the exterior space. Judging from the vertical sweeps of the window you imagine the volume of the room, the studio. The monumental inanimacy of the furniture. Vernon understood the all-conquering inanimate in a way nobody has ever understood it. The ever-victorious inanimate...

And through all this Hare thinking: why is he telling me about this guy, who is of absolutely no interest to me, when what interests me, and him too, in all likelihood, is Rosewall? It was as plain as the nose on his face that this Vernon was little other than an unconvincing and grotesque glove puppet Lynch had thrust his criminal hand into with the aim of distracting Hare's attention from the high spectacle of Rosewall.

The high spectacle of Rosewall. A monstrous shadow show. His huge silhouette propped up by enormous beams, the cut-out hook of his chin blocking out the sun on some lonely copse of Fourviere Wood, his tread heedless of the numbers, his Rosewall pack on his Rosewall back, his Rosewall stick in his Rosewall hand, his Rosewall eyes on his Rosewall...

Hare sat in the chair and hoped it might all resolve into simple saga as life in general did. Simple saga was the way life rolled for Hare. In simple, intemporal, turgid waves. They drove you ineluctably to your tombstone.

And all the while it was going on, Hare was managing to keep his eyes from flickering about in incomprehension by pinning them on the gloss of the picture. It had been a mistake.

It had been a mistake for him to trek out to this place, to accept this invitation and so find himself in the terrible suburbs in mid-afternoon, there exposed to the entire quiver from Lynch's predator bow. He heard Lynch's saliva lap and froth behind his lower gum.

Lynch. His spittle bitter as gall is bitter. His long, high rib cage. It appeared that he had fought for the Restoration, which was what they were ironically calling the disappearance of Rosewall these days; that he had been instrumental in bringing about the wheeling of events. Not that events had wheeled as with a mighty creaking of the mechanism. That had not been the way Rosewall had been hounded from the city. It had been under the cloak of night that Rosewall had slipped away. Because the balance had tipped just that millimetre further than his calculations had predicted, because certain figures had not quite corresponded to the curves of certain graphs, because a stranger's eye had not fulfilled the promises he had expected, or because…

In which case it would have been Lynch who had helped to perpetrate the hugely subtle action whereby Hamlin had been rid of its troublesome piper. And if this was the case, as the photographer Warwick had been at pains to make clear, then why was Lynch hiding out here in this construction, bleak and horrid, three-room and two-storey? But then why was Hare out here in this construction, lost in the wilds of the suburbs where Hare never ever went, and, moreover, in the mid-afternoon?

Lynch. Moving gently in that circumnavigatory manner that Hare had come to recognize as his own around the figure—comic, shadowy, looming, oppressive, distant, serious—of Rosewall. Scattering, as it were, more seed around the spot to see what fold might spring up—ten fold, one hundred fold, one thousand fold. Lynch next coming up with another anecdote of concealment to set beside the one where the Protector had shat himself stupid in the Tassin Tower, where this time hugger-mugger Rosewall was supposed to have hid in an apple tree on Fourviere Hill in Fourviere Wood, so showing himself once again as no more than a craven filcher, until in his trembling he made the rosy apples fall and so disclosed his hideaway, whereupon he scarpered with his tail between his legs, his bollocks clacking together like marbles in a pouch, he and his band of outlaws, deeper into the Fourviere Forest where his lair was even now apparently, as other stories told. And yet with his next breath there was Lynch calling him a formidable opponent. After a minute changing the expression into a sly fox, giving him once again that fable role which was so much of his costermonger's presentation of Rosewall scampering up and down the leafy greenwood lanes of Fourviere Forest.

Whereas Hare had always had him, Rosewall that is, in the steeple tower of the village church, not hiding of course but surveying the battle, so that by some silent transmutation Rosewall had become the steeple itself, a great looming shadow cast on the country, his face on the clock of the bell-tower, two watching eyes, one scanning the north, the other the south, the arms of the clock inexorably revolving to direct the movements of his battalions.

Hare, the art book still on his silly lap, looked across to where Lynch had moved away to the other side of the room where he was scouting for his cigarettes. With Lynch there was a whole strategy of deceit and thrust, diversion and counter-thrust, decoy and counter-counter-thrust.

He draws the barrel of a cigarette from the packet. He brings a flame up close, as though to tinder gunfire. He waves the flame out. He places the match down softly on the table. After his working on the cigarette, the cigarette comes to red.

SEVEN

Lynch. Shifting the conversation, even as he was shifting the coals in the grate with his poker with its handle in the form of a sword handle, to the subject of Dittmar, saying of her that she was the wife of a man.

—Who? said Hare. The redhead?

—Yes, said Lynch, knowing perhaps or feeling in his intuition that Hare had had his eye on her all along but preferred for her to fall into his lap; in any case, poking, like he was poking with the poker to see which coals had received the flame and which had not. Now they were sitting in the chairs in front of the grate. It was growing dark. The sunlight parallelograms had gathered together into a corner and then climbed away completely. Those odd coals that glowed glowed, or surfaces of them. Others were touched by pinpricks of pale orange or were still heavy black coals. Lynch's arm extending, then retiring to his socket, his torso unmoving, just the arm issuing, then retreating mechanically, as though his arm were the bloodless extension of the poker he was jabbing into the hot coals with metronomic regularity.

Hare watched the orange in the fire where it flamed up a moment and then was consumed, in the same way as Lynch was bringing to brief flame the subject or the hope of Dittmar, flaming her up and then consuming her so that Hare felt already that he had lived and exhausted the history of Dittmar, that his hope that she might provide salvation was already scorched through. He saw how poor his futile hopes were. And what did that mean he was? A poor sap. Hoping that a woman who was not much more than a redhead to him might, out of the blue, come up with salvation, simple salvation, as though from out a jam jar.

But then what was Lynch poking for amongst the coals? What was the sterner stuff of the conflagration? Vernon? Hare himself? Was that possible? Rosewall? Inevitably Rosewall. And Hare was thinking up a remark about the redhead to disavow all interest in her, actually on the point of coming out with some commonplace or other, when Lynch, who in the three hours they had been locked together in this house in the suburbs in the mid—or by now late-afternoon—had only mentioned Rosewall in footnotes or brief asides, suddenly swerved to head-on talk, changing his expression drastically from that of the bemused detachment with which he had been staring into the coals to an intense focused presence, as if no movement or twitch of poor Hare escaped him. Indeed, he had perhaps found Rosewall in the fire. A coal of him perhaps that resembled his massive granite head in the scuttle.

—Rosewall, he said, as if formally entitling the forth-coming interrogation. Hare inched his way back on the chair and rested the small of his back against the wood, composing himself as though to hear a storyteller of old. He dared hardly believe as much. The fire was not roaring. It too refused to participate in what might once again turn out to be monstrous fraud, pure deception, arch skullduggery and legerdemain, filthy lies. The fire was not roaring. It was not roaring but it was starting to lap, the tongues of light starting to overlie the figure of Lynch like so many supple slats or bars caging him, or else it was like some metaphysical rib-formation woven about him like the invisible protective shields that the ancient gods wove about their heroes.

—Did my interpretation of Rosewall's coat-of-arms interest you?

—It did, said Hare.

—And what do you make of it?

—It's impossible, said Hare.

The die was now cast.

—Impossible? How's that? Impossible?

—Gules a weasel is impossible without a bend sinister.

Lynch let out air from the back of his throat.

—Why don't you put that expertise of yours to some use, Mr Hare? It must be the only time that a heraldry expert could change the course of history. Yes. I know you're a heraldry chronicler. Gamma triple minus perhaps. But heraldry is only a minor subject these days. At least it was until Rosewall came to town and introduced the Ur-charter.

—You know I work for Wyvern? said Hare, his voice bleaching.

—Why do you think you're here with me? And why a guest of mine at the Opera Grill? It's not, I regret to say, for your sparkling conversation.

—So? What do you want to know?

—The so-called Rampant Lion must be definitively disgraced. The falseness of his claim to nobility will be a key element. As a credited Agency chronicler you have the right to produce copy. Tell me. Do you want Rosewall back?

—I don't know. What's the alternative? You've seen what's happening in the city? And he was democratically elected.

—What's happening in the city now is a state of temporary turmoil. Rosewall must be digested. The Lion must be ousted. Historians must situate him. Chroniclers must reveal him for what he was.

—And what was that?

—A tyrant.

Lynch loaded another coal onto the pile.

—The weasel is impossible, said Hare.

—Is the seal authentic?

—Yes.

—How can it be disauthenticated?

Hare looked worried.

—A seal can't be disauthenticated.

Lynch smiled and brought the sword-poker up vertical.

—Perhaps the choice of word is unhappy, but, in sum, that's what we want. We want the seal to be disauthenticated. We want people to think that Rosewall was pulling the wool over our eyes with his seal. The seal must be reinterpreted. You tell me a weasel won't work. All right, we'll forget the weasel. We'll forget the labrador, if that won't replace the lion. But what could work? In what way could this be an elaborate fake?

Hare brought his palms together and turned his mind to it.

—Gules a weasel is impossible without a bend sinister. There is no bend sinister…

—Shame, interposed Lynch. The bend sinister means an illegitimate birth, doesn't it?

—It does, but there are other, more arcane ways of revealing an illegitimate birth. A boar wearing a crown in the chief sinister, for example; or a vert or green wolf in the chief sinister. Green is the colour of the Emerald, of Venus and hence Love and the wolf in the chief sinister represents unnatural love.

—Chief sinister? Remind me what quarter that is again, will you? I never took Blasonry at the college.

—Divide the shield into four quarters. The top two are called Chief. The bottom two are referred to as Base. Dexter is right from behind the shield and sinister is left.

—So can we find a way of interpreting Rosewall's shield as false or somehow showing him up to be illegitimate? You are the chronicler, Mr Hare. Reveal the Rampant Lion to be no more than a Weasel and you assassinate not only Rosewall but the spirit of Rosewall. More vodka.

Lynch got up and went into the kitchen to fetch the bottle, leaving Hare alone by the fire-side.

—If I could find Rosewall and interview him, imagine what that would mean, said Hare to the empty living room.

Lynch was listening.

—An interview's worth more than an assassination, if it's conducted in the right way, started up the host when he came back with the bottle. As a Wyvern chronicler, you know that. Words will kill. Trap a man into using words. But lacking words, signs must point the way. Signs and emblems. Your domain, Mr Hare.

You know the story of Rosewall on the Croix Rousse Hill. He was seen there. The story was later told, only recently I might add, by one of his own men. He was on the Croix Rousse Hill, as I say. Anyway, it turned out one time that he left his men behind and advanced through the scrub. A figure came to meet him from over the brow of the hill dressed in black. In city clothes, which apparently struck the men as strange even at the time. They were watching from a distance, so they were unable to get a proper view of the stranger's face, but he was a grave elderly man with a scroll of parchment in his hand. As the story goes, the greybeard promised Rosewall to have his will then and in all things else for one hundred days, at which point his fortunes must needs wane. Rosewall apparently argued the short span, but in the end the pact was made and he returned crying out joyously to his men *now the day is surely ours and I long to be engaged*. What is one to make of a story like that?

Hare raised his eyes and looked at Lynch. Then, to disperse the moment, he sniffed a little as though he were nursing a cold. He took a sip of his vodka.

Night came on fast. It was a starry night. The constellations pointed no way in particular. They were standing on the back doorstep by now, the two of them abreast, Lynch blowing cigarette smoke again, this time into the big night, and holding a garlic sausage in the other hand. They were there as if in a prelude to a decision or departure. If there was to be a decision, it was to be Hare's. Did he want to discredit Rosewall? That was the decision he had to make. He downed his latest glass of vodka and started his initial series of sighs and tut-tut-tuts which were the prologue to all his departures. The cityscape was just beginning to move back between the plates in his brain when Lynch mentioned the gas-man.

A gas-man, he said. Coming round tomorrow. Mid-morning. Say eleven. Lynch couldn't hang around for him. Would Hare be so kind? It meant kipping the night there. There was a sofa. It opened out. Flips open like a paper-back, said Lynch, sketching the gesture with his wiry wrist. Hare nodded. He looked back up at the Milky Way. The redhead would have to wait. Twenty-four hours wouldn't make any difference to the outcome. They'll be round between eleven and twelve, said Lynch of the gas-men. Unless, of course, there were no gas-men. Another story. Like the nonsense he'd been feeding him about Rosewall signing pacts with the Prince of Darkness. Hare looked up to the stars above. Sable night, he thought. The real thing. He took his manicure out from his waistcoat pocket, began paring his nails.

The last bus from the suburbs was not an institution Hare had had much to do with. The last bus at its terminus. The big face of its headlights, the frontage of its bonnet, the small face of the driver behind his glass cabin; dusty, death-laden, waiting for the clock to touch its appointed hour. Better, the gas-man, the sofa opened out, the hum of the fridge from the kitchen, Lynch upstairs, his snores, his long body lain out on the iron-frame bed, one eye and a slice of his forehead buried in the pillow, his hollow chest and shoulder turned to blot themselves up against the surface of the bed, covering his front from all exposure, his mind careering, shuttling through the inner mineworks.

—How many gas-men will there be then? asked Hare, conjuring up the image of a number of uniformed men surrounding him suddenly as he lay outstretched on the bed-setee.

—That, I couldn't tell you, replied Lynch elusively.

—Is it gas-men or a gas-man? quizzed Hare resolutely.

—I really couldn't tell you, reiterated Lynch with a little smile. I don't know how they go around, gas-men. Maybe there's a pack of them in every van. It wouldn't surprise me.

Hare poured himself another vodka. He took a sip. He was tired. He closed his eyes for a moment. The suburbs. Tomorrow, gas-men. The fridge whirring softly. Lynch's sickle jaw chewing on a bit of sausage. He imagined his saliva sitting and gently rocking to the vibration in the pit of his palate.

EIGHT

Next, a change of air. The next week. The hotel bedroom. Back there. Hare again. Interminably him. He looks in his mirror. He is wearing his black turtle-neck. A couple of days before he'd gone shopping for another black turtle-neck. You don't have much imagination, said the shopgirl, her mouth gormless and disbelieving.

He'd looked at himself in the three-angled mirror of the great store. The triptich of Hare. His anguished constitution staring back at him from three separate points behind the fancy looking glass. There he was, sliced into quarters, the confrontation of four men, each as solutionless as the next. In the perfect light, for the perfect inspection, for the perfect examination. Suddenly arriving that glaringly propitious moment when the in-depth scrutiny of the moveables and the immoveables could no longer be put off; the Great Store and Hare adrift with all the household goods, electric tin-openers and soda-siphons, all the thick silver-plated commodities of this long-interminable life-contract.

Hare was over by the sink when Prospect pushed open the door to his room.

—What do you want this time? said Hare. Keep popping in here like a stage-devil.

Prospect was rubbing his palms together.

—The invitations are going out for Wyvern's Winter Feasts' Cocktail Party. You know that, don't you? Let me tell you that to date I haven't spotted your name on the mail shot.

Hare went back to washing his hands at the sink.

—Are you listening to me?

Hare was scratching a bit of dirt out from behind his finger nails.

—I've got a message for you from Wyvern, went on Prospect, tipping his head back to reveal his unfull throat, Hare saw in the reflection in the mirror.

—Aren't I the lucky one!

—It's your chance to redeem yourself.

—I thought the All Souls' was over.

—I'll tell you your brief.

Prospect waited for Hare to take an interest. Hare started drying his hands.

—I'll tell you your brief then

—Tell me my brief then, replied Hare with affected disinterest. Hare was looking at the sharp Adam's apple on Prospect's throat.

—A report on the Forty Notables.

—That old chestnut.

Prospect went on unheeding.

—The history of the most notable of the forty notables. Here's the list of those you should give special attention to. The Arundels and the Clarences. And Rosewall, of course.

—Of course.

Prospect handed Hare the list. Hare put it down on the bed without looking at it.

—You'll see that special comment is to be made on the supporters and crests. Lucky you're still of some use. But this is your last chance. You can be sure of that. It was touch and go at one stage.

—Touch and go? What was touch and go?

—There were some of them ready to nail you down.

—Who were?

—Wyvern has been following your case with some interest.

Hare lowered his head, looked down to his hands.

—Just get this piece out. And make it good. That'll be atonement for you.

—Huh, was Hare.

—What do you know? We might even pay your hotel vodka for you.

Hare gazed out of the hotel window and looked within his heart for a true picture of what he saw there.

The city was a hall of distorting mirrors where men and livestock herded together. It was sometimes difficult to tell the two apart. Livestock advanced down one street and then the next, the way it was whipped or the way its fancy took it. In this, it was no different to men. Also, the same thoughts passed through the rambling brains of livestock and man: how to find a way down this maze of streets.

Hare saw himself with the rest. Trailing along happily enough, smiling idiotically from face to snout, snout to face. Undifferent to them, but feeling himself to be different. Engaged with them in the same labyrinth, but feeling he was bound some place, following a private itinerary known only to him.

And if that's the case, then how do you explain your lack of initiative, your passivity? Waiting for Lynch's suggestion before finding an idea for action, a way of behaving faced with paralysis; experiencing desire for a redhead only when he's told it's appropriate. More Cardinal Sins. Add them onto Pride and Vanity and take a look at Hare's oval soul then. The isolated stains are spreading and pushing towards each other. Soon the whole will be grey. Hare, this is the beginning of evil. This is how it starts, a life of sin.

NINE

Lynch and Warwick were seated at their usual table when Hare trudged in. They called him over, Warwick with elaborate, beckoning gestures of his arm and great winds of laughter.

—We were just talking about you, said Warwick.

—Sit down, said Lynch. What'll you have to drink?

—A vodka.

—What we were saying was that you must spend half your life freezing your arse off on Little Pizzay Street waiting to get in here. Now is that the truth?

Hare flushed at Warwick's remark. Warwick went on.

—Imagining you we were. Out there in the blizzard.

—Yes, said Hare. Particularly cold tonight.

—Come rain or shine, said Warwick, starting to rap the table in his glee. Lynch was lighting up a cigarette.

—Yes, was Warwick, poking Hare with his index. You're getting to be quite a regular. Why, we ought to get a key cut for you!

Then, laughing and turning to Lynch: Eh, Lynch?

—Why not? said Lynch, blowing out blue smoke.

—It certainly would be convenient, Hare hastened to point out.

—It would make a nice Winter Feasts' present, said Lynch, smiling behind the bars of his fingers and cigarette. What are you doing for this year's Winter Feasts' anyway? Got anything lined up?

—Nothing special, answered Hare.

Was it true Wyvern was going to exclude him from the cocktail soirée this year? Hare had toiled for many a year to get onto the Wyvern Cocktail List. Now he'd chucked it all out the window. There was tragedy for you. No place to go for the Winter Feasts'.

Warwick sat back on his chair, blinking, looking from one to the other, from Hare to Lynch and back again. Lynch was joking surely. He wouldn't offer Hare a key to the club, would he? Hare was moving his finger slowly around the rim of his vodka glass.

—That would be handy, he said. Especially at the moment, as I'm looking for a place to stay. It'd be handy knowing I could pop in here at any time of the night.

—What's happened to the hotel, asked Lynch.

Hare shook his head in distaste.

—Unsatisfactory service, he said after a minute.

—Yeah! said Warwick. I know what you mean.

—And you're looking to move out, are you? asked Lynch.

—Thinking of it, said Hare, nodding and seeming to meditate on the tempo of the nods. Giving it some serious thought.

—Hotels are all much alike, aren't they, concurred Lynch.

—They sure are.

—I've always wondered why you haven't got yourself a little apartment somewhere, said Lynch. So much more pleasant.

—Yes, well, I'm beginning to wonder myself.

—I'll tell you what, Lynch went on. Why don't you come round to my place for a few days? You know what it's like. Small, but there's room enough.

That's a booby trap invitation if ever I heard one, thought Hare, accepting the invite and thanking its donor warmly.

—That certainly would be ideal. Thank you very much. Events have kind of forced my hand, you see. Thank you again. A few days grace, just fine.

—Don't mention it, (Lynch). And now I want you to meet a friend of mine, and he called the redhead over to the table. It was just the kind of ploy you might have guessed at from him, proving they were all in it together, Warwick, Lynch and the redhead trying to make a tomfool of him. She came smartly over as though it had all been rehearsed and sat right next to Hare. It was black-berry all right.

Hare could see Warwick out of the corner of his eye slouched in his chair scrutinising the proceedings, leering slightly as Hare thought, though he didn't care to check up on the details too closely.

—Do you know Dittmar? he'd said.

Hare had grunted.

—Of course he does, was Warwick's comment as he sat up in his chair.

The redhead was wearing an emerald green pullover with a heavy golden chain about her neck.

—That's a pretty chain, noted Lynch immediately, taking the medallion between forefinger and thumb to feel its calibre. He rubbed it a moment and looked the redhead in the eyes.

—What's it of? asked Warwick.

—St Anselm, interjected Hare.

Warwick took the information in with a nod of his lolling head.

—What expertise! laughed Lynch.

—The traditional St Anselm pose, explained Hare. The boar-skin and pig's bladder, and the blade held at hip level. The patron saint of the Levellers. Also if you look closely—may I a moment?—you will—unless I'm very much mistaken—notice the emblematic beacon at his shoulder.

—Bravo, was Lynch.

—I always wondered what it was, said Dittmar, her eyes lighting up. I always took it to be a taper.

—A good guess! flattered Hare. It's true. It does look rather like a taper.

When he glanced at her he noticed the freckles which seemed to have grown darker since he last saw her. They overlaid her face like a soft, providential sprinkling, even dappling the watery pink lips.

—Mr Hare shows a very lively interest in Rosewall, mentioned Lynch, intoning as though to bring intrigue to a canter.

—But that's only natural, was Hare answering back. Whatever we say about him, he was quite a character, and glancing across to Dittmar for her verdict.

—No, but I only mention it by way of introduction, because Dittmar was quite an intimate of the fellow. Weren't you, my bird? said Lynch in a gentler voice.

—Hardly, said the redhead. Or if you like I was the woman who betrayed him. That's the way they like to put it.

She motioned across towards Warwick and Lynch.

—Only in joke of course. In reality, there were many women, as well as many men, who betrayed Rosewall.

It was only later when Hare found himself alone with the redhead for a moment that she undertook to explain to him her betrayal of Rosewall. She leaned over towards him so that he saw the texture of the eyeliner on her lids.

—That was just a little joke you know, about me betraying Rosewall. It was the only time I ever came into contact with him. He was walking his pet labrador.

—I didn't know he had a labrador, said Hare.

—He was walking his pet labrador and it was raining, she went on. I knew it was he. By this time he was well known. It was at the time of the Livestock Bill. Anyway, he asked me if I could hold on to his animal for him while he went into the shop.

—What kind of a shop?

—It was a hat shop. I said I could, but he was in there so long that I ended up handing it over to a woman who was waiting for her sister. That was my betrayal of Rosewall.

She smiled.

—What was he doing buying a hat? asked Hare, not a little put out by the idea that Rosewall should go around with a hat *and* a labrador. It was not at all the idea he had formed of Rosewall. What if he moved his arm around the back of the chair and pretended there was a bit of fluff on her poloneck and plucked it off? He sat back in his chair for a moment.

—What happened to Rosewall? he asked.

—I don't know what happened to him. Did anything happen to him?

—I don't know, said Hare, pretending to think seriously about the question, looking at the gold of her heavy chain. They do say he's mustering men.

—Who's that? she answered with a little laugh. Warwick. You don't want to believe anything Warwick says!

Then, in a sudden movement, he brought his hand up from round the back of the chair and brushed her cheek lightly with his forefinger. It was a kind of elaborate twist he made with his wrist and elbow. He was wrong to have tried to do it all in one move.

—What are you doing? she cried in a voice suddenly acute.

—I was just knocking a bit of pastry off your cheek there.

—How dare you! she said. She was furious. Her ears were scarlet. She was struggling to get up from the chair without pushing it back, her hands splayed on the table to help her up.

—It's gone now, he said. It was just a bit of fluff pastry...puff pastry...

—I don't care what it was. I haven't eaten any pastry, she flamed.

—That's odd. I was just brushing it off with the back of my hand.

Hare re-etched the gesture in the air for her benefit.

—I could see very well what you were up to, she cried. She was standing now and gathering her bag strap shoulder-wise across her torso. It brought out the swell of her breasts.

—I don't know what you're getting into such a fluster about, reiterated Hare as she about-turned and strode away, her buttocks rippling voluptuously behind the high-quality woollen fabric of her skirt.

He had been wrong to try and accomplish it in one movement. That had been his error. What he should have done was first take his hand out from the lattice of the chair-back and place it down on the table, and then with a graceful elevation of the arm pluck off the offending and fictitious bit of fluff, at the same time excusing himself and explaining the intimacy with a brief word of the type: *just a bit of fluff. I'll have it off in a jiffy. Not to worry your pretty little head about it. There now!* Instead, it had been that ugly arabesque whereby he had almost clipped her one on the nose.

In any case, he had other things on his mind right now, didn't he? For instance, his hotel bill. For instance,

Prospect and Wyvern. For instance, saving his skin. If he didn't watch his step he was liable to find himself lugging that mattress around with him, just like his fictitious brother a few months earlier. He was hardly likely to let a redhead insisting on her pastry-free diet trouble him overmuch.

The smartest move he could make now would be to get out of the hotel before the youngish hotel receptionist could pick up on anything. What was he waiting for? Hadn't Lynch invited him? He could clear out of the two-star hotel. If the youngish man got wind of him, he'd say he was going off for a couple of days.

What! In the middle of the night?

He was driving through the night with a friend, a Mr Lynch. Mr Lynch had been instrumental in ridding the city of Rosewall and his cronies. They hoped to reach their destination by morning. They were bound for...—now where could it be?—they were bound for the humble village that was the seat of the Rosewall dynasty, now an accursed sight on the tourist route. How did that sound? They were looking into the myth of Rosewall's nobility which, it appeared, was turning out to be as bogus as the fellow himself. They were looking to find the evidence which would score him definitively from the list of the forty notables. How did that sound? Yes. Hare would come clean at last. Hoist his true colours to the mast.

More than that, it was suddenly clear what was required of him. That was how it was with Hare. Things suddenly clarified. He'd bluster around for weeks on end, not knowing what he was about. Then, with a gust of wind the fog would lift and he'd find himself embarked on a road leading somewhere. An interview with Rosewall, for eg. The scoop of the century, for inst. How about it? What would Wyvern say to Hare tracking down the

Rampant Lion and procuring that killer interview that Lynch had spoken of?

When he got back to the hotel he took his square suitcase out from the cupboard and put it down on the floor. After a moment's thought he stretched out on the bed, setting his head down softly on the bolster. It would be the last time.

PART THREE

FUTILITY

TEN

Hare's search for Rosewall was to be undertaken, so Hare repeated to himself, on the most systematic of bases. No stone was to be left unturned, no witness of the events to be left uninterrogated. Witness: Lynch. Witness: Dittmar. Witness: Warwick. The first batch whose accounts would surely lead to others. Hare was resolved to come to terms with the skein. If not untangle it, then at least find its end.

He opened up his personal journal and dated it. The red hotel curtains were drawn to. In his head the fragments encrusted themselves, then detached themselves from his game careering consciousness. His lust for Dittmar, his mistrust of Warwick, his curiosity about Lynch, his disdain of Prospect, his rejection of Dittmar, his mistrust of Lynch, his humiliation, his dependence on Lynch, his rejection of the Agency, his jealousy of Prospect, his needs, his fear of the youth of the youngish man. Then there was that other one, Gloucester, who'd never really spoken. Gloucester the Engineer. And above it all, like God the Father in some sacred painting, Rosewall enthroned, his trusty labrador on his right-hand side, his ireful brows (beneath the broad-brimmed hat) bent on those below. The Opera Grill. How it all fitted into reality. Or how it never quite fitted. His fictitious brother with the mattress. Where would he be now if he existed? In another land, holding down a job? When the globe spun, did it still fling reality out that way? How looked the lie of the land? And the lie of a man, his angle of recline, built, as he was, into his fortress by wife lover friends esteem money despair hopelessness inevitable loss terror. And he, Hare, short-arsed Hare, impostor and eternal third-party, who now tasted his own palate in his mouth, having arrived at that time in life after which you begin to taste your own flesh, he, short-arsed Hare, if it came to holding down a job, how would he hold one down? With a half-nelson or a Boston crab?

When Hare arrived at the arcades that surrounded the Opera House it was eight o'clock. The sun was up and out in the sky. The tickets for the evening show were on sale. It was Balajo, a medley of exotic tunes with dancing and masquerades, all done in the oriental style. Lynch was filing forward with the rest. In his long black raincoat he inched forward in tiny steps. His face was drawn and saturnine, the skin peeling a little on the triangular expanse of the nose. Hare moved in next to him as he approached the box-office.

—You want to fit in? asked Lynch, his concentration still fixed on the *papier mâché* plan of the seating arrangement that was propped up against the kiosk window.

—Nothing for me, answered Hare, as much to the people queuing behind as to Lynch. I want the number of the redhead.

—Two places slightly to the left, third row, if not second, said Lynch as he arrived for his turn. OC23 and OC25 if you have them left.

Hare watched his long hands placed delicately on the wooden table of the box office, as though they were extended to let the varnish dry on his nails.

—Dittmar, said Lynch as he turned away in mild triumph, the two tickets in his hand.

—Yes. Her.

—What do you want with her? Not that it's my business.

—I've got a few questions to ask her.

—When are you moving into my place?

—Whenever it's suitable.

—It's suitable at once.

—I'll move in tonight.

—I'll expect you.

They were standing on the steps of the Opera House. Hare had put one foot up on the top step and the other on the next one down, which meant that he had his knee up flexed before him like a useful piece of furniture to rest your hands on.

—Was she in the club last night?

—Yes. We had breakfast together a couple of hours ago, answered Lynch.

—Perhaps she'll be sleeping if I phone her now.

—I'll give you the number anyway, shall I? he said after a moment. He was watching traffic. I'll note it down for you on this little pad with the address on the other side, eh?

—It's not too far from here, is it?

—You could walk it in twenty minutes. It's on the other side of the plaza. One of those streets leading off it. It backs on to Haberdasher's Yard. You know it?

—I've heard of it.

—It's where the rag trade workshops are.

—Thanks, said Hare.

—Just before you go, have you thought about the Rosewall blason?

—Yes. I've had an idea about it. I'll let you know tonight.

Hare went off clutching his piece of paper preciously in his overcoat pocket.

Hare felt he wanted to prolong the moments of his possession of the scrap of paper before he actually undertook to act upon the information it contained. He walked jubilantly through the streets towards the plaza enjoying the shop windows, the cafés with their early morning clientele, the waiters hoisting up the metal coulisses that protected them from night prowlers, a whole strip of pavement loaded with excess ice from the fish market, the rag trade carts picking up the day's produce from the wholesalers before the onset of the inner-city traffic, the pie taverns starting to bake, the street-cleaners finishing their nightly round. Rounding a corner he came upon a van with its backdoors swung wide open on the hinges, and behind the van door the butchers standing together in their hooded blood-stained gowns. Then he looked up to where there were three men in a house, two at windows letting down buckets of debris on a pulley system to a third standing on the pavement. Together they had it roped in, the house, even at eight thirty in the morning, and if the house were a mammoth face—Rosewall's for instance—its eyes were gashed and the interior of the head made roomy. They were putting the house to rights.

As Hare approached the plaza he felt his indeterminate state of contentment changing, shrivelling, becoming transformed in his pocket as he clenched it, so that when he picked it out to look at it once more, even as he crossed the plaza, his intention being to locate the exact spot where he was (it appeared) bound—Haberdasher's Yard—he understood, it dawned on him, that his indeterminate content was now indeterminate unease. Daylight had transpierced the paper, carbonised the unsophisticated glee. Ungainly truth! How to come to terms?

So that when he saw the road in question he stopped. Charity Street. It was a long perfectly straight roadway traced through the pancreas of the city leading to the sulphurous railway yards that lay at the base of the inner-city precincts, which stood up like a man between the two arms of the river. It was deserted at that hour.

Hare walked on the wrong side of the road, sinister-wise, marching swiftly as if preoccupied by a business of some nature. He looked at the tenement blocks on either side of the road with theatrical contempt and cursory speculation, scanning them as though he were a potential purchaser. It was in case an anonymous onlooker should catch him in the act of approaching Dittmar's house. His lust humiliated him. This house would perhaps subjugate him definitively. If his fictional brother had seen him stepping shamefully along, what terrible retribution would follow?

When he arrived at the appropriate level of the street—he saw the alley that led to Haberdasher's Yard sidling off out of the corner of his eye—he straightened himself up and scratched the dandruff off his shoulders in case it had pitter-pattered down there.

It was the basement flat. He went softly down the metal steps. The door to the coal shed was open like a flap, which he tried unsuccessfully to re-establish flush. The flat was quiet. He listened against the door. Behind the frosted glass of the window there were colours: eddies of emerald green; the glow of mustard; a hard biscuit-brown bar. He swallowed and brought his knuckles to the door.

Immediately he knocked a figure was formed from the colours behind the glass. The figure loomed and stag-gered towards the door. It was a man. Hare prepared for what it would be: the opening of a door and all that that implied.

—Dittmar, said Hare.

A small fox-eyed man was standing behind the door, unhandsome, rubbing his tousled hair with a towel.

—It's for you, said the man, turning back into the room.

—Are you the husband? asked Hare, raising his eyebrows out of politeness.

—No, I'm the brother-in-law, he said through the towel and the fierce rubbing.

The brother-in-law walked off over the mustard carpet, his head hidden by the towel, his arms and hands straining furiously as though this were the histrionic climax to his next transformation, the last one being his assembling from behind the frosted glass.

Hare stepped into the apartment and gave a last clawing to the possible dandruff on the shoulders of his jacket.

—Come in, said the Fox. No, I'm the brother-in-law. Husband to the sister of the woman you're looking for, who'll be out of her bath in a moment. Sit down.

—Thank you, said Hare and placed himself in the large heart of the soft green cushion of an armchair; one of the emerald green suite. He sank irreparably in and his legs lay before him like metal legs, helpless before the drift of his bulk. He shifted his eyes feebly in his head while the rest of him was entertained by the foam which had come for him, confiscating those other parts, limbs, torso, bum and all that. He was spread-eagled on the rapids many miles downstream by the time Dittmar came padding out onto the mustard carpet in a dressing gown.

—I was expecting you, she said.

Hare was looking up at her from the green armchair. He nodded his head and neck stiffly on his shoulders.

—How's that? he said after a moment. Did Lynch phone you?

—No. But I knew you'd end up chasing after me.

—I'm not chasing after you. It's information I'm after.

—Oh Yeah! she said.

She was watching him out of the corner of an opal eye.

—Have you met my brother-in-law? she asked, introducing him with the palm of her hand. Hare looked in his direction. The Fox looked up from his glossy magazine. It was W W WOMEN, a Wyvern production.

—Who do you think let him in? said the brother-in-law. The cat?

—My brother-in-law married my sister. My sister left to go off for a weekend. That was a couple of weeks ago, she explained.

—And does he live here? asked Hare tentatively, not knowing whether to lower his voice or not.

—For the time being.

The Fox was flipping through the coloured mag, the towel round his shoulders, pretending not to listen to the conversation. Hare was trying to extract himself from the armchair

—Can we talk alone? he said when he had perched himself on the edge of the cushion.

—What about? she said, looking at her bare toes which she was winkling and twinkling, Hare saw.

—Rosewall.

—What can I tell you about him?

—Probably more than you think, said Hare making to get up and lead the way into another room if there was one besides the bathroom. There was another door opposite the bathroom door, though it may well have been the airing cupboard.

—What do you want to know about Rosewall? asked the Fox who was wearing a pair of blue-framed spectacles suddenly. Yet another transformation.

—Is that your bedroom? Hare asked Dittmar, deliberately ignoring the brother-in-law, thereby hoping to enter into complicity with the redhead.

—It's the pantry, she said.

—Let's go in there, he said and led the way in.

She followed him, somewhat bemused.

—What do you want in here? she asked.

Hare was pushing the turnips back to find a place to sit on the floor.

—Any place'll do, he said.

—This is where I keep my provisions, she replied, looking round at the vegetables and tinned foodstuffs in puzzlement as though for the first time.

—I can see as much, said Hare, brushing off a turnip with the balls of his fingers.

To his astonishment she was clearing a place on the floor to join him amongst the vegetables.

—Well, said Hare when she had set herself down lithely beside him on the tiling. He was holding the turnip deliberately as though it might be acting as the symbol of some element in his proclamation.

—I'd like you to understand one thing clearly, he started. What I want from you has nothing to do with what was said between us before—a misunderstanding, I might add—which was brought about by a third party whom I've now learnt to distrust, thanks to your advice. I'd like to take advantage of this moment, by the way, to apologise for any unnecessary anxiety that any of my actions or statements might have led to on your part. Needless to say, I hope that unfortunate and, personally I believe, trivial misunderstanding won't stand in the way of my present attempt to broach a completely unconnected subject. As I said, the subject of my present inquiry is Rosewall. Look upon me as a kind of Private Eye, working for my own reasons, impelled by motives of my own, whatever they might be. Personal motives.

Dittmar was smoothing down the towelling of her dressing gown on her thigh. She had folded her legs discreetly underneath. Her neck was elevated. She watched Hare seriously with nut-brown eyes. Her eyebrows were level extending to a splendid T-junction with the top of her nose.

—I don't see how your motives can be personal, she said without changing her posture in the slightest. Her limbs did not perform perfunctorily like Hare's did. Her words just came out; bare, simple, plain words with the meanings that words were meant to carry. With Hare language was undermined by the unbridled play of arms and hands, the twitch and tic of the animal, a whole substratum of denial aimed at the verbal layer, hacking into it, leaving it blackened. It was as though the storm reared up and took his words even as he uttered them, causing them to be exercised, flung downwards or rained on, windswept or drenched.

—What do you want with Rosewall? she was asking now.

—I have my own interest in Rosewall. It's personal.

—What? Did you know him?

—My brother knew him.

—The one you're looking for?

—Yes.

Hare nodded his head solemnly.

She was visibly dissatisfied with his explanation.

—He left the city. That's all I know, she said.

—Who? Rosewall or my brother?

—Rosewall. I've never even set eyes on your brother, have I?

—Perhaps the way I'm putting it doesn't suit your cast of mind, proffered Hare, his head tipping somewhat to the left to get a better look at her cleavage.

She looked round at the pantry to reassure herself of the concrete objects. She seemed to wonder what had caused her to sit upon this pantry floor.

—I have the impression you're not really saying very much, she said after a moment's reflection.

—I'm telling you what I can, answered Hare smartly.

—I followed you in here to be away from my brother-in-law, she replied challengingly.

—To be out of earshot?

—Just to be away from him. He so invades my world. It's just pleasant to be in this pantry for a moment... I so rarely come in here.

She seemed to realise how unhinged all this might sound and that it was Hare who was unhinged, not her, after all. So she shrugged her shoulders a little as though to excuse the inadequacy of her idea.

—Because I don't want you to go thinking I particularly wanted to follow you into this pantry.

—I was thinking it might be your bedroom or else an airing cupboard. I hardly thought it would be a pantry.

—If it had been an airing cupboard, how could we have got in? she asked, bemused, half to herself.

Hare smiled knowingly.

It was so remarkable that she should be here in this close confined universe of the pantry that she was desperate to find the reasons why she was there or at least the connection between the old, everyday world and the sudden leap into this odd space. It appeared to her that she had been unavoidably plunged into this pantry with Hare, as though lowered down in a dumbwaiter into an odd and tacky nether world. Perhaps it had been just one instant of charm in the unattractive man that had tumbled her into this space.

She was trying to wield herself back to view the scene with her habitual clarity. What had happened now was that her foot found itself extracting warmth from Hare's calf. It seemed to her such a brusque and physically difficult action to shift it elsewhere amongst the litter of vegetables and conserves. She looked over to the pantry door. It was sealed tight

—You must ask Lynch about Rosewall, not me, she said, slapping her own instep as though a prelude to hoisting herself up, but not getting up, waiting for her strength to return or for the situation to stabilise into one she might understand.

—I mean to question him too, answered Hare. It's cool in here, he then said after a pause.

—We must get back in the sitting room then, she said.

—No, in a pleasant way I mean it's cool, corrected Hare, and took her wrist to prevent her from getting up. He let go of it at once.

She was watching him with mistrust as if he had tricked her. In that moment she was ugly to him and he sensed the possibility of conquering her. But by looking away shyly at the imminence of such an outcome it was lost and she started back on her regained territory.

—Your search for Rosewall's just a subterfuge. It's not Rosewall you're looking for at all, she said with a wicked curl of her lip.

—Who else could I be looking for?

—What about that brother of yours?

—I have no brother. He was invented.

She looked puzzled.

—You mean he's just a half brother? she said.

—No. He's invented. He's not even half a brother. He doesn't exist.

The redhead was unsure whether or not she should look shocked by Hare's sudden disavowal of his brother.

—Why on earth invent such a thing? Do you think we care if you have a brother or not?

—I was an only child, said Hare.

—What's that to me! (her lip curling monstrously).

—I'm only telling you to explain that I can't be looking for my brother because I don't have one.

—Then there's only one answer.

—What's that?

—You just want to bother me.

—That's just where you're mistaken.

At this moment the pantry door swung open and brother-in-law popped his head around. Hare moved back to let the door fully open and let the Fox in, as though it were the most natural thing in the world for the three of them to be jammed into the pantry, it being the leisure room, like the T.V. room in some two-bit hotel.

—He wants to know about Rosewall, said the redhead.

—Any information would be much appreciated, added Hare looking up and fixing on a smile.

—I can tell you about Rosewall. What do you want to know?

—Where is he?

—In the city.

—Where?

—In hiding. He hasn't left the city. He was a puppet usurper. People are starting to understand that now.

—Are they?

—The Council Chamber set him up to put through some strong measures. Then he stepped down. He'd served his purpose. His job was done. He drifted out. He'll materialise again in a few months. Take my word for it. In the main stream this time.

—Just like his wife'll materialise, said Dittmar.

—She'll be back.

—I wouldn't count on it. She's gone. She's not coming back. I'm her sister; that's all. You think by talking to me you'll get in touch with her, but it doesn't work like that.

So saying she leapt up and scrambled out of the pantry, kicking some turnips Hare's way in the process. The Fox remained stationary, his back against the door, looking down at Hare. He had combed his hair over into a neat quiff.

—As I was telling you, he said. Rosewall was a puppet chief-of-state. Certain legislation had to go through. It was the only way. What do you want with him anyway?

—I'm just curious, that's all, said Hare, wondering where Dittmar might have got to. She'd be dressing, he thought.

—It's no use pinning your hopes on Rosewall, went on the Fox. This situation won't change in a hurry.

By the way he looked down at Hare sprawling amongst the vegetables it could almost have been that he was referring to Hare and the pantry fare.

When he finally got out the bathroom door was open and the scents of pine forest bath foam were wafting through the flat.

—She's gone, said the Fox and sat down to his mag. He perched his spectacles on his narrow-bridged nose.

Hare said: I'd better be going myself, and went.

It was a Sunday. Haberdasher's Yard would be empty, he told himself. As he was in the vicinity, it seemed reasonable to take a look at the yard where the group that had agitated for Rosewall's coming to power—the Twelve—had preached. The Twelve had represented a remarkable confederacy only a few weeks ago. Where were they now? He entered by the brick alley that led from Charity Street. The yard was still. The flat cobblestones were strewn with rags and cardboard boxes. On the blind brick wall that faced him, high up, was what remained of a Rosewall poster. It was now almost illegible, Rosewall's head almost completely eradicated by the intemperies of the climate, persisting only as a blackened round scorched on the paper. One of the corners of the poster was peeling and flapping lightly in the breeze. He looked about him. He was hemmed in by the high brick walls of the yard. There was a wooden dais standing beneath the highest of the walls. Hare thought instinctively of the gallows.

Just at that moment he heard the sole of a boot on the cobbles behind him. The brother-in-law was standing there, now dressed up in a duffle coat.

—I saw you slipping down the alley, he said, his features suddenly animating as if switched into operation.

—It's odd you living just here, said Hare.

—Not me. I don't live here. It's your friend and her sister. It was their place. Anyway, someone's got to live here.

—Do you know if she went to meetings?

—She told me she went to one or two. To see, I suppose. You would, wouldn't you? Living on top of it like that. Of course, whether this lot—he gestured to the empty yard—knew it was all fabricated or not, I mean that Rosewall was being handled by other powers, that's anyone's guess. Who's to say? Maybe it was all a monster theatre put into operation by those handling the business.

Hare was pacing up and down the yard.

—There's many others coming round to my way of thinking, you know, went on the Fox, his eyes trained on Hare. He watched him earnestly for a few moments before relaxing his face muscles and looking up to the oblong of blue sky directly over his head. Pigeons were flapping across the light space to the dark surround. They found crannies in the wall and lodged there.

—The day is slow, slow, slow, said the Fox. You know, it's still only nine o'clock. Have a cup of coffee, if you want. I've got a toaster.

—No, no, said Hare. Where did Dittmar go?

—To bed, said the Fox.

—Where's the bedroom?

—Not here. To another flat. I don't know where she goes.

Hare stamped his foot on the cobbles. The sound echoed and was immediately smothered.

—Do you want a cigarette? asked the brother-in-law?

—No, I don't smoke. I'm going anyway.

He went. The Fox trailed down the alleyway after him, watched him for a moment progressing down Charity Street, then went down the metal steps.

ELEVEN

When Hare arrived with his two suitcases, the square hard-cornered one and the soft-bellied modern one, he found Lynch sitting next to a plant that he had just acquired, or so he explained. He had left the door open and was waiting for Hare. The plant with its large oval green leaves was fanning him in the stirring of the air from outside.

—You're not cold? said Hare, struggling with his luggage over the threshold.

Lynch remained seated next to the plant, the forefinger and middle finger of both hands spanning his legs just above each knee.

—I'm airing the place, he said. I like to do it once in a while. Do you like my plant?

The verdure was nodding sedately beside him like a friend.

Hare said it wasn't bad and how much was it?

Lynch said it was the first plant he had ever bought. He'd never liked the idea of sharing with a living thing; a fridge was bad enough with its infernal thermostat going off and on without you all through the night.

—As I say, said Hare. I shan't be imposing on you for long. The time it takes to get my ideas together.

—That can take quite a time, said Lynch smiling a little.

—No, if you'll give me a week or two's grace, that'd be just the ticket, went on Hare.

—A week or two, repeated Lynch. That's time for someone who's searching actively. Are you searching actively for a place?

—Thinking about it.

Lynch fingered the leaves of his plant and turned his eyes to it. It was an astonishing green. It issued from the soil in two thick stems which were strapped together at various points on its upward extension. After three feet the stems produced branches of the large oval leaves which seemed to hover in the air uplifted by their own strange buoyancy. There were two levels of leaves bouncing gracefully on their invisible cushions. Lynch in his armchair was about the same height as its topmost leaves, and he turned to it as though consulting with a dwarfish mediator.

—So what are your plans? he said, suddenly turning to Hare as Hare was looking round the untidy room.

—Oh! said Hare. To find a place. That's foremost in my mind.

Lynch nodded for a moment.

—You're very interested in Rosewall. Am I right? he said, touching his plant once more.

—I must admit, answered Hare grinning sheepishly, he does afford me a certain fascination.

—One might almost say you're on a Rosewall hunt. We've all noticed the interest you take in him.

—All?

—All of us. Myself, Dittmar, Warwick, Gloucester.

—Did Dittmar ring you?

—She rings me all the time. But tell me, do you have business with him, with Rosewall?

Hare laughed into the air.

—Perhaps we can close the door, he said. It's getting chilly in here.

—By all means, said Lynch and motioned. Hare shut the door and turned back towards the man and plant.

—No, he said then, making a big fuss of getting himself settled in the inferior armchair opposite Lynch. No, it's not that. I'm curious about Rosewall, where he might be just now, and that's it.

—So, tell me about your ideas for the coat-of-arms.

Hare clapped his palms together to steady himself a moment.

—Rosewall, he said. Rose. Wall. In theory. Of the family Rosewall. But what if our Rosewall were not of that family. What if Rosewall were a corruption. Road's Way, for example. Or Roat's Weal. Or Rose, as in rise rose risen; Well...

—Well?

—Well. I looked into this. I think we can get away with Road Sward. Road as in Road. Sward as in Greensward, meadow, field. There was a family Roatsward. There still is a family Roatswar. It should be enough to reinterpret the coat-of-arms to explain the confusion and create a crossing of paths in the backward of time.

—A crossing of paths in the backward of time no less.

—That's a quotation from the Crest and Blason Almanac.

Lynch smiled.

—And where do you publish it?

—There's only one place where it will get through uncensored. The Herald. It's the only paper where my pass gives me priority publication access, the only place the Qual-Gods don't touch it.

—Qual-Gods?

—Quality-gods. They check everything to see if it's in keeping with the Wyvern philosophy.

—Whatever that is.

—Yes. But I can get by the Qual-gods on blasonry in The Herald. It's my only priority publication access.

—The qual-gods will be sleeping, will they?

—It's not that they sleep. It's just that they don't think a threat can come from certain nooks of the edifice. In any case, you can be sure it'll be taken up by other large circulation news-sheets and will get through the net in some of them because other people like me only with higher priority publication levels will push it through.

Lynch smiled and touched his packet of cigarettes.

—If ever you knew those different pools of light and shadow, I mean the blind spots of the qual-Gods, I know a man who'd be willing to pay large sums of money.

—Nobody knows that. Least of all me. Wyvern is a series of cells. The only time I ever meet other Wyvern representatives is at the Winter Feasts' Cocktail Party, and that's something I fear I won't be attending this year.

Lynch nodded.

—Well, he said. Here the rules are simple. Keep the place as tidy as I do. That's not asking for much. Don't overdrink my vodka when I'm out. Treat the place like your own for the time you're here. More or less, that is. Your bed's the flap open bed. You already know it. Retire, necessarily, after me. If I'm out late, go to bed when you want. I'll do what I can not to disturb you when I get back. And that's it. Any queries?

—I'll publish the article right enough. Be sure of that. But what I really want to do is find Rosewall and interview him. What do you think?

Hare fixed Lynch, as well as he was able. His eyes were small and it was difficult to know you were really engaging with them.

—Rosewall's dead, said Lynch.

—That's not been proven to my satisfaction.

—It has to mine, replied Lynch and chose to terminate the conversation.

When Lynch went up, Hare flipped open the bed settee and stretched out amongst the clutter of the living room. The green plant eyed him carefully, stirring slightly as though to remind him of its vigil.

Hare had insisted on keeping his two cases by him for the first evening. They lay a few inches from the settee like domestic animals, hopelessly out of place in the alien landscape of the living room. Lynch had proposed taking them upstairs and stocking them some place out of harm's way. Hare had told him not to bother as he'd be rooting in them in the night. They were, after all, his only worldly possessions. Lynch said it was good having so few because it kept a man mobile, a quality he hoped he hadn't lost himself, this tumbledown house notwithstanding. It was a necessary quality these days, he went on to say.

In the middle of the night Hare was awoken by a scuffling on the stairs. It was the kind of noise you might get if you held a microphone up to a mouse hole or the kind of noise Laurel and Hardy might make when trying to be stealthy. He made out the figure of Lynch ascending the stairs bearing some heavy burden. It was one of Hare's suitcases which he was transporting back to his lair. Fortunately, it was not the hard-cornered one, which meant that his secret journal had not, for the moment at least, fallen into his landlord's hands.

Hare turned his thoughts to his antagonist. If Hare could be sure who his antagonist was, the matter would be simpler.

The Enemy can take many forms. It can come clothed in light like the Bright Angel. It is typical of the Enemy to introduce sound thoughts only to waylay the spirit, but then, little by little, he tries to achieve his own purposes, by dragging the spirit down to his secret designs and corrupt intents. There is no force on earth so savage as the Enemy in the ever-growing malice with which he carries out his evil plan.

The Enemy is like a woman, weak in the face of opposition, but strong when not opposed. In a quarrel with a man it is natural for a woman to lose heart and run away when a man faces up to her. But, on the other hand, if the man begins to be afraid and give ground, her own vindictiveness, her wickedness and her viciousness overflow and know no limit.

Hare had given the redhead too much ground. He had lacked the courage to face her with the arms of a man. Instead, he had listened to her and allowed her to choose the terrain of the encounter. There had been no charge, no will in his venture. How could it be crowned with success? His fortitude had been tested and found, like all the rest, wanting.

TWELVE

Warwick lived in a curious brick building whose doorway gave out onto a flight of steps that led from the base of the Croix Rousse hill up towards the natural shelf that marks the point from which the clustered houses of the city begin to fall away and the scrubland begins to encroach. The house was one of a row of packed terraces lurching up the hillside. It was a block conceived more for the heart of the many-dimensioned city with all its distorting mirrors and brutal chimeras than for the edge of like desolation. Such, at any rate, were Hare's thoughts as he mounted the giant staircase holding the cold metal rail with his ungloved hand.

Night was falling. Warwick had invited him round for an evening drink. Hare paused a moment in his ascent. He saw the air change to vapour as it came out of his mouth. He turned. The lights of the city were already glimmering. His low-level view of the city was comparable to that of a bird of prey when it swoops down to snatch its victim. That would be the angle of vision of the city that greeted Warwick every morning when he turned from pulling the front door to. A few feet higher up the stone steps and the dark metal rail stopped. A mud track led the way over the brow of the natural shelf. It was perhaps down this descent that until recently livestock had been led into the inner precincts of the city.

Warwick was wearing an ill-fitting pullover which hugged his torso so tightly that Hare could make out the form of the rib-cage hooped about him like some coil of rope round Harry Houdini. At the point where the cage gave way to the soft padding of the belly the lungs were causing the acrylic pullover to swell and shrink as though it were the breathing tissue of the man. Warwick's bony wrists seemed to extend interminably up into the narrow funnel of the sleeves like two long bundles of faggots.

—Come to see a man about a dog? he said and started to laugh.

He slapped Hare on the back and ushered him into the oblong room.

—You don't mind sitting on a hard-backed chair, do you? he said.

He placed it down in the centre of the room facing the window as though he had come to watch out for something in particular. Hare took up the post as his due.

—It's a long walk up, said Hare.

Warwick's long body was arching over by the drinks cabinet.

—It keeps me in form, replied Warwick coming over with a bottle of vodka and two glasses.

—Everyone seems to know my tastes, said Hare with a smile.

—We've noticed you like a spot or two of the stuff.

Warwick tapped the label with his forefinger.

—This isn't the best stuff on the market but it does the job. It soaks up the excess anxiety, I say.

Hare nodded as he watched the colourless liquid filling up his small glass.

—We'll drink the first pony down and then we'll talk, said Warwick when he had taken up a position. He was still standing. His long brows arched. Hare looked up at him and thought he would be hard put to find anything more sinister.

When the first glasses were set down on the table Warwick pulled up a chair for himself.

—Now you'll forgive me if I come straight to the point, he said.

He had placed his own chair at an angle to Hare's so as not to block his guest's view of the window. Hare was forced to twist himself a little on the hard-backed chair.

—Word has it, commenced Warwick, turning the high vaults of a cheek towards Hare. It was a habitual gesture of the gaunt host to turn first one side of his face, then the other, towards his interlocutor.

—Word has it…that you have it in mind, and not only in mind but in deed too already, to hunt down Rosewall. Is this true? Answer yes or no.

—Yes and no, returned Hare watching the contours of sinew in Warwick's cheek.

—We won't go into that, but hear me out. So: yes, you do. Good!

He paused and brought the ends of his fingers together.

—A noble venture! One that would serve the needs of all concerned. And we are all concerned, believe me. And, as you say, it's only natural us wanting to know what became of him. So, that being the case, let me make you a proposition. I'm prepared to go half with you. Fifty, fifty! We split it right down the middle!

Suddenly Warwick was smiling and his palm was stretched out towards Hare as though to settle the bargain there and then.

Hare looked towards the wings of his dilating nostrils.

—We split what right down the middle?

—The manhunt! said Warwick.

Hare searched a cranny for his eye-beams.

—In what way? he asked.

—The costs.

—I wasn't thinking of paying out any great sums of money. I'm just asking a few questions, making a few inquiries. And, in any case, it's no manhunt.

—You know what I mean.

—I don't know that I do.

—This is a task that needs to be executed properly. It's owed to all concerned. Now, I spoke to Lynch about this and he agrees with me entirely. I broached the subject and he's backing us up all the way to the hilt.

—He hasn't mentioned anything to me.

—Perhaps he hasn't but he agrees with me entirely.

Warwick smiled gruesomely and showed Hare his left jowel.

—A full-scale operation, he went on. We mount it together, you and I.

He tapped Hare's kneecap with his raw knuckles.

Rosewall, thought Hare. Perhaps if he viewed the great spider Rosewall in the bulbous eye, recognition might come, a revelation of the whole scaffolding and quaking structure of his—how to put it?—estate.

—But wait a minute, he said. What about the redhead? It's not true what you told me.

—What's that? replied Warwick, starting back in his chair and frightening Hare with the intensity of his astonishment.

—She never said that about me at all.

Warwick was pouring the next pony of vodka.

Hare repeated: She never said that about me at all. That I was all right.

Warwick thrust the glass into Hare's hand.

—Suffice it to say, began Warwick deliberately, that I was doing it for your own good.

—For my own good! I don't need you to tell me what's for my own good and what isn't.

—Cheers! Come on! Drink up!

—Are you listening to me?

—I've heard your opinion on the matter. It just so happens that I believed and I still do believe it to be the case that Dittmar has an interest in you. I believe that most firmly.

—And I'm sure she doesn't.

—How can you know such a thing?

—She told me so herself.

—So what! Do you think she's going to drop into your lap like...

Warwick looked for an image.

—...Like... a jackpot in the penny arcades. You've seen her. You've seen the body on her.

Hare swallowed distastefully.

—Women like that play hard to get. It's in their nature. And what's more to the point, would you respect her if she did drop her knickers straight out? Could you, could I desire a woman like that? That's right! Now I'm talking desire.

Warwick scratched his face all over, flushed with excitement. Hare looked out of the window to the image composed half of the night and the facade of the terraced block opposite, half of his own reflection. A brief sketch of some ghostly Warwick figured within the frame. He was watching. His long musculature arched tensely towards Hare, ready to swoop.

—Mark my words! said Warwick. Now listen. Wednesday I'm working with her at the Lynch studios. You know where they are. We're doing another advert. You can watch. Come in the back way. I'll leave the door open for you...

—Now listen...

—No! You listen to me. You can watch! We're there all morning. Wednesday next. Now let's get back to business. How to conceive of this our enterprise. How are you going about getting information on Rosewall?

—I'm just asking around. And that's one thing I find funny. You know where she lives, this redhead? In a road that backs onto Haberdasher's Yard. I find that suspicious.

—Did you mention it to her?

—I mentioned it to her brother-in-law.

—What did he say?

—He said somebody has to live there. I told him what I thought about that in no uncertain terms. I reckon she must have known Rosewall. Whatever, she knows more than she's telling.

—Exactly. You see my point.

—What point?

—It's why she's fascinated by you. You unearthing Rosewall like that. That's why she's attracted to you. That's simple psychology. That's the way it works.

Hare pursed his lips to give the matter some thought.

—If anyone knows about Rosewall, it's got to be Lynch, said Warwick.

—Why do you say that? riposted Hare fiercely because it was what he had always feared.

Warwick turned his high cheek towards Hare as though anticipating further questions. In truth, it was his ear, well waxed in the pit, that he presented his guest. He went on to speak, however. His small eyes now visible from a three-quarters angle darting to the right, where Hare observed him, and to the left, the window and the framed third party of the night beyond.

—I remember the week before Rosewall was elected. I never saw Lynch so fraught. You couldn't speak to him. He snapped my head off more than once, I can tell you. Because he knew what was going on, what would happen if Rosewall came to power. Rosewall was already taking control of a majority.

—In the Council Chamber.

—Behind the Council Chamber. The men for whom the Council Chamber members stood. The rich financiers of the private armies. As Lynch explained to me.

—And how did he take control of the financiers?

—He had his tentacles everywhere. He invaded the Council Chamber insidiously. And then Rosewall was brought to the fore. The rest is history.

Hare was looking at Warwick curiously now. He had the impression that Warwick was some kind of clumsy sub-species of Lynch, aping his every word and thought, fired with the same enthusiasm he might have had if the thesis were his own, whereas it was clear that Lynch was the ventriloquist behind this giant dummy-play.

—I hardly dared go out in the streets that first week. Gangs of them roaming the streets with truncheons and clubs. It was anarchy. And sure, I'm a big fellow, you'll say. I can look after myself. And I can too. But that's not much help when your dealing with gangs of them.

—The private armies?

—No. Thugs. Handpicked thugs paid to keep the order. Because news had got out about Rosewall...

—But he was elected democratically.

—News had got out about what he was going to do once he'd manipulated the votes and hoodwinked the people. They panicked. Natural enough. I panicked myself. I stayed at home. Here. I kept off the streets. I stayed here and panicked. Do you blame me? And then things went back to normal. Until Rosewall disappeared. Then it was another normal. Or another abnormal. And the rumour went round Rosewall was out.

—What had happened?

—The million crown question. Search me!

Warwick was fidgeting with his vodka glass, balancing it on the back of his thickly veined hand.

—Someone must know, said Hare.

—The way Lynch put it, started Warwick, leaning across. Rosewall was sacrificed by the financiers. A pawn on the chessboard. No more than that. And Lynch could know. He's not telling, mind. Not straight out. Because he was part of the negotiations, a consultant he calls himself, between the private armies, the financiers, the members of the Council Chamber. That's the way I see it. That's my own personal view of the matter, you understand. He was a conciliator and an unconciliator. Conciliating here, unconciliating there. Planning it all.

Warwick scratched his flushed, excited face.

—For his own ends, he added. His ends and Gloucester's ends.

—Gloucester?

Warwick looked about him fearfully

—Beware Gloucester the Engineer.

—Why should I beware Gloucester?

Warwick looked down to his feet and repeated himself:

—Beware Gloucester.

Hare let the silence settle for a moment before picking up again.

—What ends anyway?

Warwick smiled. His face broke into another element. It was the prelude to a remark Lynch had not vetted.

—I reckon he has plans. He must have. One kind or another. Otherwise why care if it's Rosewall or the next man. After all, someone has to wield power.

—He must have interests, said Hare. Money somewhere.

—Vested interests.

Hare downed his next pony.

—Now, said Warwick, revealing, Hare felt, far more than he ever had. My idea about Lynch—do you want to hear it?—my idea about Lynch is that he does have interests, he does have interests somewhere...

Hare waited, perched on his hard-backed chair, for the rest of the idea. But that was it. Warwick had sat back in his chair and was straining to twist his back round it like some sinuous plant-life, staring out of the window or, rather, into it, for it was a zone of commentary on the conversation, mirroring it and sending it back all mixed up with the oily night.

PART FOUR

CONTRITION

THIRTEEN

A ROSEWALL and NO ROSEWALL

Startling new revelations are bringing to light the monstrous swindle that is just one piece in the jigsaw of so-called Rosewall's mysterious rise to fame. So-called Rosewall? Indeed, for Rosewall was no Rosewall at all, but Grimsbelt.

Eight generations ago the ancestor of the present Rosewall engineered a huge switch that brought wealth and notoriety to the lineage. The modest family of Grimsbelt, tallow chandlers in the village of Nolton, eked out its meagre existence much as any other family of commoners of the epoch. Its joys were few and its miseries manifold. Unto them was born a child—a daughter—of a strange beauty. Jackel by name.

The ancestral home of the Rosewall's was situated in the same county as the humble abode of the chandlers, no more than 30 kms from Nolton. At this time the ball given by the nobles of the region would be an open invitation to all the county, and it is more than conceivable that the childless Rosewall's should be struck by the strange beauty of the Grimsbelt family.

The Rosewall's of the time were aging and clearly looking for a way to continue the line. The custom in the forty notable families was for the name to be passed down through children of either sex, so the choice of a girl was no impediment to their scheme. A few crowns would have sufficed to pay off the Grimsbelt family, already saddled with enough offsprings. Twelve of them!

Ever since Rosewall's decision to resuscitate the Ur-charter and all that it represented experts have been worrying over the question of the Rosewall supporters, the supporters being the pair of figures that stand one on either side of the shield to uphold it. The supporters suddenly appeared on the shield eight generations ago at the time of the adoption of Jackel. Dexter of the shield stands a Phoenix or Demy-eagle emerging from flames gules, to illustrate the miracle of the birth of an offspring. Sinister occurs the unofficial story, but the true one: a jackal and about its loins an ermine gown that is too big for it. In the claw of the jackal a round which has always been taken to be the medallion of office, but which now is revealed to be no more than a simple crown coin, the emblem of the sum paid to gain dread entrance to the now disgraced House of Rosewall.

Hare had to go into the city centre to pick up his copy of The Herald. He set himself down at the Opera bar and examined the article. It was totally uncut. He ordered a sniff of vodka and reread it. He certainly knew how to produce copy when he wanted. And even the headline was his. In The Herald he was untouchable. The sub-editors just read through for typing errors. They wouldn't dare touch his actual text. And look at that: *Unto them was born a daughter...* Quite a find, a turn of phrase like that. In the normal course of events Hare would have been due for a promotion, as he saw it. Of course, that was all shot now. This article spelt the end of his relationship with the Agency, he knew that much.

Across the square from the Opera House was advertising hoarding with a large 10 metre x 6 metre poster of the redhead in the dusty heavily furnished room as photographed by Warwick. She was wearing the red knickers and a red pullover and was sitting on a chair arching back to pick up an orange on the floor. In arching back she revealed a strip of pale stomach between the bottom of her pullover and the top of her knickers. The photograph had been given a soft-focus feel and looked as if it had been taken in a slight mist, as though there were an early-morning forest outside the casement windows. On the heavy wooden sideboard in the background to the portrait were a number of stuffed animals: a fox; a kind of hamster; a large bird. Propped up against the sideboard were two swords and a blunderbuss.

The poster was an advertisement for a chocolate breakfast drink, BREAKOCHOC. The baseline read: Waking up to the world!

Hare was busy examining the composition when he felt a tap on his shoulder. He looked round. Prospect was stationed behind him.

—Good morning, said Hare, who was feeling quite jolly.

Prospect didn't smile.

—I presume you're responsible for that, he said, motioning towards the opened tabloid on the tabletop.

—Investigative journalism, said Hare proudly. Moreover, the Rosewall supporters are the theme of the article, just as you requested.

—Maybe. But the interpretation is hardly the one we asked for.

—A man has to feel free in his work.

—And Rosewall, who was elected in a free vote...

—Where is he?

—Wyvern washes its hands of you, Hare.

—I knew as much.

—And I fear that may not be the only retribution.

—What do you mean?

—The Agency doesn't like its plans being sabotaged by some gamma triple minus pen pusher.

—What retribution are you talking about?

—Alpha plus retribution.

Hare got up from his table folding The Herald under his arm and leaving a crown in the ashtray.

—And don't think you can quit the hotel without paying the bill either.

—I've already done it.

Hare was walking across the Opera Place with Prospect at his heels.

—And where are you now then?

Hare put his finger to his lips and winked at Prospect. He felt good, really good. In one god-given moment a tram had appeared from nowhere, the doors had opened and Hare had leapt onto it.

FOURTEEN

Given the furore, which would inevitably be let loose by the article, it was deemed advisable, both by himself and his landlord, to spend a few days in the house and avoid the treacherous trip into the centre of the city. The material details of their common life were laid down formally.

Hare was to look after the basic stocks of provisions. Fruit and vegetables, dairy products, sugar and salt, tea and coffee, a supply of soups and tinned produce, cold sausage: all this was Hare's domain. The basic alimentary needs. Lynch would bring back a piece of meat every evening. This was considered the wisest ploy, as the city meat auction was, as everyone knew, the place where the best cuts were to be found.

Every morning Hare put on his mac and went out to the local farmhouse to pick up eggs and milk. He was soon a familiar figure shuffling in and out of the market stalls of the fruit and veg shelters, examining the greens, the rosies and the russet apples, the espagnolos and the blood oranges, the fleshy, the plum and the sweet tomatoes, handling the various orbs, turning them in his palm with the expertise of one apprenticed in the metier. He was on the look out for good onions for a cheese and onion pie. He'd promised Lynch to rustle one up one of these days.

The woman who kept the stalls treated him with deference. *Mr Hare* they called him. They kept him informed as to the bargains of the day, the flux of the prices. *You stopping long at Mr Lynch's place?* they asked him. *Not that long*, he invariably answered before toddling off with his wicker basket. Now and then he looked out towards the expanse of the fields and the church in whose bell-tower, it was said, Rosewall hid or else surveyed the Battle of Tassin.

Lynch would ring up every day to tell him at what hour he might be expected back. *Having a hard day?* Hare would ask him. *I'm keeping busy*, Lynch might respond in that oblique way of his that Hare was almost growing fond of.

Hare always tried to tidy the place up as best he might for the return of the breadwinner after six o'clock. Lynch came in the back way unostentatiously, always with a package under his arm; a pound of mince it was the first day. Later delicacies that Lynch fetched back from the meat auctions included a panfull of thick pork chops, a stretch of dark streaky bacon, a clutch of long beef sausages and a couple of handsome brown steaks which lay snugly together in the fryer as the pair (Hare and Lynch) watched together, waiting for the moment when the blood began to ooze up to the surface, the moment when Lynch, prize carnivore that he was, liked to plunge the steak fork in and carry them off to the two plates, immaculate white and bark-shaped, which were laid ready for the slivers of lustrous flesh.

When dinner was over Hare took the two plates over to the sink and washed up while Lynch smoked his long evening cigarette. *My long evening cigarette*, he used to say. Usually it amounted to four or five.

Shall we retire to the sitting room? Lynch would invariably suggest after Hare had dried the pots and pans off the draining board. Lynch didn't like to see crockery draining.

As he led the way into the living room Lynch never forgot to snatch up the vodka bottle. Nor did Hare forget to snatch up the two squat vodka glasses, which were never washed and sat constantly on vigil on the wooden kitchen table. They took up their places in the two armchairs in front of the fire which Hare had taken pains to keep going throughout the day, and if Lynch happened to make a remark of the kind *It's a nice blaze* or *it certainly is roaring*, Hare would smile inwardly and take it as a personal compliment, on his appearance or the taste of the cheese and onion pie he never made.

In the morning when Lynch went out to work—it would normally be around ten—he left Hare a cup of tea by the flip-out bed-settee. Hare waited till Lynch had gone before he opened up his eyes. He didn't know why. As though Lynch might reveal himself in that moment. Or was it that Hare was afraid to be looked on as a supine man by another man, and that man Lynch? Or because he did not know how to play the act of waking up? The fact that Lynch continued to make the cup of tea and place it down by the settee seemed to imply that he suspected Hare's slumber was no more than counterfeit, though in the evening the subject was never addressed. In those moments when Hare was pretending to sleep and Lynch was flitting about the morning house as though in a trance, Hare came closest to vision. It came as preface to the day. And when Lynch slammed the door shut, he flicked up his eyelids. The day, the real one, began.

One morning, as Lynch was placing the cup of tea down beside Hare's bed, he spoke:

—I saw the article, Hare. It's fine as far as it goes, but it doesn't get us that far. What we really want is something on Gloucester.

Hare's eyes remained closed. Lynch sat down at the table and went on:

—Gloucester comes from a noble lineage, Hare. And nobody has ever spoken of that. I'm leaving you an envelope with the details of his shield on the table. I'd like to see what you can do with it when I get back this evening.

When the door slammed Hare got up and went over to the table. In the envelope was a clumsy drawing of a chevron cloven shield with a fire-breathing lizard called a salamander at the base and three henchman's axes in the upper half on an azure background. The two supporters were a Hawk passant dexter and a Panther Sinister. Above it the crest of Royal Office, and at the base of the shield a motto: Executioner of Tyrant and Restorer of Order.

EXTRACTS FROM HARE'S PRIVATE JOURNAL

Keeping clear of town centre for a day or two. Chance it might snow. Heard on radio bomb placed just outside Opera House but never exploded. Talk of creating a new rump Council Chamber, but not much chance of it getting anything through. The Twelve that supported Rosewall seem to have disappeared into thin air, although one was spotted in the centre by the new shopping precinct wearing a hood and gown. Upon being challenged that he was one of the Twelve he denied it most vehemently. Apparently, he was challenged on three occasions by independent witnesses, so there is no doubt that it was he. At the moment of the third and most aggressive challenge the siren went three times to indicate a bomb scare and in the general panic he slipped away.

I am devising a set of exercises to rid myself of all irregular attachments. The aim is to overcome myself and regulate my life on the basis of a decision arrived at without any unregulated motive. The question is: how am I to regulate my life securely?

I have devised a structure for my design. Forty days are to be assigned to the exercise. The forty days are divided into four periods of ten days. The four periods are headed as follows:

1. Present state.
2. Past action.
3. Ideal for Future.
4. Preparation for future action.

The form taken by each period of ten days:

One hour of meditation per day plus a practical undertaking.

The meditation to consist of
   a) Two preliminaries.
   b) Five Headings.
   c) A colloquy.

One hour is the minimum. In fact, must complete more than one hour per session, as in this way I will get used to not only resisting the enemy but routing him completely.

Example of preliminary: one of the bodily senses (taste): Feeling completely the taste of the present. The taste of recent aliments still at large in the mouth and upper digestive system, the taste of the air and its dust or dirt, the taste of my self (the decay of teeth and presence of flesh and blood).

Example of Heading: The hotel room (necessarily in the second period of ten days being a part of my past life). The arrangement of furniture in the room. The feel of the counterpane when I lay on it. My physical weight within that room at that time. My fears and temptations: fear of hardship, sense of shame, sense of guilt at not producing copy (be careful not to overload each heading. Remember there are five headings plus the two preliminaries and the colloquy per meditation).

Colloquy is a verbal presentation of an aspect of the meditation. Dwelling on the meaning of each word. Various readings (e.g. a word per breath or else use of different pitches and registers of voice).

Apart from the daily meditations there will be points of stock-taking. Stations in time and space where the day is reviewed for a moment. Times:

On getting up in the morning.

On the toilet.

After lunch.

Sitting by the blaze with vodka.

During evening walk to the Rosewall steeple.

These stock-taking stations are separated into two varieties:

1. The brief recognition of myself in my context.

2. The more protracted moment which can take the form of a physical feat (e.g. Holding my breath for protracted periods of time or else taking deep breaths in particular rhythmic series (two deep breaths followed by three shallow breaths followed by two deep breaths etc etc).

Note: the first ten-day period to be particularly concentrated on contrition and inner distress with special attention paid to the Triple Sin of Inadequacy, Indecision, Inaction.

I begin to see Lynch's scheme. Here is proof, if ever I needed it, of his attempt to gain power. Gloucester as Sovereign. The Royal Crest can mean nothing other than this. The Azure background which is the badge of Noble Lineage. And what does the motto mean? Executioner of Tyrants (presumably Rosewall) and Restorer of Order. As for the Salamander. Gloucester the Salamander. This is a new one on me. There is no trace of a Salamander in the Heraldic records as far as I know. What new breed is this then? Gloucester the Salamander. And how am I to participate in their scheme. How can I participate in their scheme? Discrediting Rosewall is one thing. But helping to hoist Gloucester into his place another.

I remember Rosewall in the schoolyard. This is a remembrance that came back to me in a dream the other night. Otherwise I have little or no recollection of him. No recollection. He's a matt shadowy surface in my brain. In the dream he was not much more than that. He was bending over tying his shoelace. I saw him from behind. I knew his name for some reason. There was no reason why I should have known him, as he was three or four years my senior. From behind, his humped body was like a boulder with granite of his shoulder blades and knees. That's my real remembrance of Rosewall, which I try to disengage from the rest.

Sometimes I feel what I really need is a physical instruction. When the body is constrained, the mind must need follow. To this effect I have laid ready a birch rod I found in my wanderings on the waste fields beyond the market stalls. Who knows when the need will come for me to take the rod and inflict just retribution upon myself?

FIFTEEN

When Wednesday came Hare caught the tram into the city centre. He got off the stop before the studio. In his conscious mind he wasn't sure he'd turn up, although he knew there was nowhere else he could go. He walked quietly to the studio.

—Mr Warwick?

—What's your name? asked the receptionist.

—Hare.

—I have a note for you.

The receptionist produced an envelope.

Hare read: Hare, I'm in studio 27. Come straight up. It's on the second floor. I'm leaving the door ajar slightly, so you'll be able to get in without disturbing us. When you get in, try not to make much noise. There's a screen directly behind the door. You'll be able to watch from behind there. Happy hunting. Warwick.

Hare tried not to think about the note. He just went up the stairs to the second floor and along the corridor to studio 27. The door was slightly ajar, as the note had promised. Hare stepped quietly in and pushed the door to behind him. By a slight motion of the head Warwick acknowledged Hare's entry. Hare held his breath.

—Shall we get down to it? said Warwick.

The redhead breathed out.

—Do you want some music on? asked Warwick.

—No, let's not, she said.

Hare could see her from behind. She was wearing a rust-coloured dress buttoned up high at the neck. The heating in the studio was full on. Hare unbuttoned the top two fasteners on his shirt.

—So, today it's Waking up to the World again, said Warwick.

She sighed again.

—Second in the series. Here are my instructions.

Warwick took a sheet of paper out of his trouser pocket.

—I don't know why we couldn't do them all in one go, said Dittmar. It'd make things a lot easier.

—You know what they're like. This is top secret, mi dear. They like to sound out the reactions before deciding on the next sequence. Do you want a drink?

—No. I'll be all right.

—So. I'll read it to you, shall I? That way, you'll get it straight from the horse's mouth.

Hare pricked his ears for the instructions.

Warwick cleared his throat.

—Chocobreak. Sequence 2. Same Room. Stuffed animals facing the other way. One sword and blunderbuss propped up against sideboard. GIRL on sofa. Apple in her hand. She holds apple up to the light and is examining it. She is no longer wearing the red pullover or the red knickers. The pullover is on the floor at the foot of the sofa. The knickers are on the sideboard wrapped around the stuffed hamster. We imagine she has thrown them there. She has a broad red scarf draped about her. The same red as the discarded pullover and knickers. The scarf is worn like a sash diagonally across her torso, so one shoulder is fully discovered. The sash comes down to her navel. Her legs and lower parts are thus fully discovered, although because of the angle we do not see any pubic hair.

Lighting… etc etc. The lighting I've already set up.

So. Get the picture? Ready when you are.

Hare swallowed.

Dittmar proceeded to unbutton her dress. Warwick cast a furtive glance towards the screen. Hare looked down towards his own feet. At the top of his angle of vision he was aware of the shifting shadows of Dittmar as she was taking off her dress. He lifted his head. She was just letting down the dress round her ankles and stepping out of it. She was wearing white underwear. Her hands came round to her back and unfastened the bra straps. Hare focused on the grain of the skin between her shoulder blades. She strained her shoulders back. The bra disappeared and left the expanse of her broad back and well padded shoulders. Then she stepped out of her knickers. Warwick was fiddling with his camera.

—Ready for action? was Warwick, looking up to survey her.

How obscene it was for Warwick to be examining her nudity like that, thought Hare. He was almost tempted to step out from behind the screen and stop this thing before it went too far. But he didn't. After all, his own position was far from virtue itself. How would it look? It would be as if he'd turned up as a simple voyeur.

—Wrap the sash round, said Warwick.

Dittmar moved across the room and took up the sash. Hare got a profile view of her orbs. Flat stomach; tight little bum; and on top of it all that freckled face he knew. She really was something. It annoyed Hare once again to think of her performing for this giant monkey Warwick.

—Now take the sash left to right and wrap it across. That's right.

Hare watched her wrap herself into a bend sinister gules.

—Look over there towards the toilets, said Warwick and commenced snapping with the camera.

Hare focused on the back of her neck, which was exposed on the left side. Also visible from Hare's acute-angle vision was a sliver of the averted left eye, a whirl of the left nostril, the tuck of an armpit, the profile of the left knee and shin.

—All right. Pick up the apple and hold it up.

—Where? she asked.

—Hold it up with your left hand. A bit higher. Lift your head up a bit. Tip it back a bit.

Hare watched her perform.

—Could you let a few strands of hair down in front of your face?

Dittmar ran her hands through her hair and pulled a few strands down.

—And look at that apple with admiration and...

Warwick looked for his word. Hare couldn't stand much more of this.

—And ...desire.

Hare wanted to leave now. His breath was turning rancid in his own lungs.

—Do you mind if I put the transistor on, said Warwick. This atmosphere's a bit too dirge-like. Not charnel enough.

Warwick switched on the local pop station where a guitar riff was reaching its final screeching moments.

—Coolness, said Warwick in a vulgar attempt to dictate the atmosphere. Hare had started to sweat, he realised. He hoped his throat would stay moist enough to avoid the sinful cough.

—Pull that sash down a bit, honey, said Warwick.

Dittmar rearranged it.

—Let's get that love-light in your eye. This is supposed to be erotic.

Hare looked back down to his shoes. His body sounded deafening. The blood rushing and the wax in his ears churning.

—Open your legs a touch. Let's get the idea of something.

Hare opened his mouth to exhale a sigh but smothered himself. The music on the radio changed to an oboe and electric lute madrigal.

Warwick put his camera down and moved over towards the sofa. Hare thought for one terrible moment he was about to pull the screen away and expose him, but he stopped in front of Dittmar and knelt down in front of her. Hare strained to see what he was up to but from behind it was difficult. There was the sound of the sash being ruffled and the clicking of Warwick's tongue against his upper teeth.

After twenty seconds or so, it occurred to Hare that Warwick could not be rearranging the sash, he must be doing something else. He must be touching her. He must be. He had to be taking her breasts in his huge ungainly hands. What else could be happening? It was clear to Hare. That's what he was doing. He was rubbing his hairy finger backs around her nipples and she was letting him. Hare felt dizzy. She was letting him. She was just sitting there and enjoying it. Hare was just about to open the door and storm out into the corridor when Warwick moved back over to his camera. The expression on his face had not changed. Perhaps he had been arranging the sash after all. But what had taken him so long?

Hare allowed himself a swallow of saliva. He was hot. The heating in the studio was full on. The radiators were just behind him. He was sweating under his winter clothes. What with the odours Warwick would be wafting across, the redhead wouldn't notice another pair of sweaty armpits in the place.

Had Warwick really been touching her up? When Hare brought his thoughts to bear on it, he found to his horror that he was getting an erection. He felt sick with the idea of it. Warwick playing the role of lead male in his sexual fantasies; what an idea! He couldn't see much now. Warwick was snapping away. He strained his neck to get a better angle on the redhead. Not much doing. He rocked back onto the soles of his feet. He closed his eyes. Warwick kneeling before her. His huge head up level with her breasts. What Hare wanted was for Warwick to hold her by the neck, pull down that sash, push her back onto the sofa, for her to emit sounds from the back of her throat, sighs of total relief, that she should be taken by such a brute. Hare himself was no more than a dwarf compared to Warwick. In what way could he compete? In what way participate in the ravishment of Dittmar? It would be a sorry performance. With Warwick at least he could watch. And as Warwick bore down on her, drawing back her only half-struggling limbs to the pose of total exposure—Warwick was a veritable Hercules—she would cry out, say things. What would she say? She'd egg Warwick on, ask to be taken. Then she'd mention Hare, laugh at him, the very idea of him, the very notion that he could have designs on her (he was such a dwarfish oaf and she was a fantastic creature). Warwick and Dittmar would laugh together. Their complicity would find Hare for its butt. This really excited Hare; the idea of his humiliation and the chance to watch her from a position of total security, focusing just on Dittmar, her shapes and movements, but aware also of the shadow of Warwick working on her, bringing her to intense pleasure, moving her machinery for Hare's eager eye.

Hare opened his eyes. The session was going on. He'd seen enough. He eased the door open and escaped to the safety of the corridor.

What a degrading spectacle to be tricked into hiding behind the screen and observing Warwick at work. At work indeed! That Dittmar girl behaving like a common street harlot. A nest of debauchery, the whole affair!

And yet, I must confess, the spectacle does afford a certain fascination. Interesting to see the mechanics of it all. Warwick and the redhead, the way they communicate. The pair of them covering up their uneasiness as best they can. Covering up with their unsophisticated methods. Pretending it's all in a day's work. I dare say the most baroque of scenarios pass through Warwick's little Brontosaurus brain. I wonder who he takes himself for with his camera in hand taking those pictures of ostensibly a naked girl. The girl's put together well enough, I suppose. Though she's nothing to write home about. The usual formation of limbs and appendages, common to all females. I must admit I'd be curious to have a closer look, from the front this time, get a proper look at her stripped facade, to see in what way it might vary from the norm.

There has been news of sightings of Rosewall. In the lowest of the popular rags, I hasten to add. One tale in particular struck me. It happened in the Croix Rousse Gardens. The great aunt of Rosewall was weeping there and was approached by a man she supposed to be one of the municipal gardeners, who asked her why she was weeping. She said that it was on account of her nephew who had disappeared. She didn't mention the name Rosewall in case the gardener turned out to be against him. But when she turned fully to him and the gardener raised his head, she saw who it was and moved forward to touch him. Master, she said. But Rosewall stepped back and told her not to touch him or to speak of the sighting to anyone. She went joyously away and, we can only assume, promptly sold her story to the highest bidder. In the newspaper there is a picture of her laughing with her two thumbs up in triumph, presumably celebrating the jackpot she just earned herself rather than her nephew's return from the dead.

There are so many stories of Rosewall now. He has already infiltrated into a children's nursery rhyme as the new bogeyman.

Over the seas for many days
Won't come back if the sunshine stays
If the sunshine goes then touch the wood
Rosewall comes if Rosewall could.

I heard this as a child's skipping song as I was out at the market looking for onions for the cheese and onion pie.

I now use the simple doggerel of the verse as one of many bases for my breathing exercises, first breathing after every word, eking out the verse; then, trying to say each word as long as possible, taking care to let the word fade with my dying breath; then, as quickly as possible, all in one breath. It is amazing the different notions that come to me as I go though these exercises. Breath which is life transmutes the notions of the mind.

Sometimes I take up the birch rod and beat myself over the shoulder in a rhythmical swinging motion with my right arm, keeping in time with the rhythm of the verse. That's the point of it. It's hardly flagellation, just a regular swishing motion. And it's true that the smart that my back feels on the contact of the birch makes sense of the words.

Over the seas
For many days
Won't come back
If the sunshine stays
If the sunshine goes
Then touch the wood
Rosewall comes
If Rosewall could.

Let the inventory now be made.

The sin of Fear. The sin of Presumption. The sin of Inaction. The sin of Cowardice. The sin of Desire. The sin of not being able to sit still. The sin of following his own conscience. The sin of interpreting one moment as revelation and not seeing it as a trap thrown by the Enemy. The sin of being on the short side compared to Lynch and anyone else you might care to mention. The sin of not knowing what the fuck he was about. All those sins. Some of them mortal. All of them mortal. Venials didn't get a look in. Spears to the side, the lot of them.

And Grace? Was Grace likely to show up? Did it come from out the blue? Or did you feel its approach? Had Hare felt anything? Hare, had you felt anything?

And when it came, poured onto the soul, as he had always imagined, like from out a gravy bowl, gluey and white like béchamel sauce, did it really make the soul spotless and did it really make a simple smile possible again on a face grimaced with so many sins?

SIXTEEN

When Hare got back to the suburbs after his trip to the studio, night had fallen. Lynch was waiting at the kitchen table, his empty plate before him, the stain of gravy upon it. He was sulking.

—You went into town today then, he said.

—Yes, said Hare, squeezing round the back of Lynch's chair to get to the sink and pour himself a glass of water from the tap.

—I thought you were cooking a cheese and onion pie, said Lynch.

—Yes, said Hare. Couldn't get the onions.

—There were onions on the market.

—Not the right ones. I can't just use any old onions.

—I ate from a tin. That's all there was in stock.

—A tin of beans and sausage.

—Did you leave me any?

—I was starving when I got in.

—It was a tin for two.

—I was starving, Hare. I was expecting a cheese and onion pie. I didn't bring any meat back.

—Yes. I'm sorry.

—And there's nothing for tomorrow lunchtime.

—We'll open a tin of soup. There's that.

—Soup? What soup?

—Oxtail, said Hare.

Lynch looked at Hare.

—We'll have a bowl of oxtail soup, said Hare again, trying to summon up enthusiasm for it, for Lynch's sake, to stop him sulking.

—Oxtail, said Hare again, and as an afterthought he added: Made from the tails of city livestock.

—Show me the Gloucester article, Hare, said Lynch, fixing him.

Hare stuttered that he hadn't written it.

—You'd better hurry up with it, said Lynch, who was twisting on his chair to get a look at Hare head on. Tempus Fugit.

Hare said he wasn't going to do it. He said it was absurd. A Salamander indeed, he said. Whoever heard of such a beast on an Azure background! Hare said it was out of the question, it was impossible, it was more than his reputation was worth.

Lynch said nothing. He turned back round on his chair and stopped trying to look Hare fully in the face.

Hare just saw the profile of one of Lynch's eyes over his shoulder, the lashes fall and rise as he blinked, and for the first time it came home to him that any discourse Lynch might have on Rosewall or anything was surely to cover up some wound and trauma of his own.

The next day, which was the beginning of the end, Hare saw a little more. Lynch was revealing himself, or perhaps exposing himself, for with Lynch it was more in the nature of an obscene act. The tin of oxtail soup sealed it. In no uncertain terms Lynch wanted him out.

It was raining. Hare did not know Lynch. Hare knew nothing about him. It came home to him. It was the crux. Lynch was unknowable. It was suddenly the gravest commonplace of his imaginings on the subject. Lynch was opaque. Lynch was a sinister, vivid, omniscient, dreadful personage. Hare feared him. Hare was shorter. There was no doubt about it: compared to the lean Lynch, Hare was a short-arse.

Hare came down the stairs. He was watching Lynch in the kitchen through the slats in the banister. The stairs twisted a little. This was a crooked house. What was Hare doing in this crooked house? He slipped into the kitchen and stood by the sink behind Lynch's chair. Lynch shifted his gaze. He was chewing on the inner rubber of his lip.

Hare sat down.

—Open up that soup now! said Lynch.

Hare got up. He went over to the stove. Lynch started rolling an orange around in the palm of his long hand. The rain was dashing its way in onto the tiled floor. Hare looked out to the uncurtained windows to the scrubland at the back of the house. Suburbs.

—What soup is that you're making? asked Lynch.

—Oxtail.

—Doesn't go with orange?

—No. Tomato's the one that goes with orange. You should have told me. I'd have opened up a tomato.

—Close the door.

Hare got up to close the door.

—As I think I told you before, said Lynch, as Hare was pushing the door to. I don't believe it's possible for Rosewall to be mustering men. It's vulgar chit-chat.

Hare looked at his own highly manicured hand on the doorknob. He hadn't even mentioned Rosewall. Lynch was going on:

—He was granted a hundred days. The hundred days passed. Rosewall with them.

—And what government shall we now have? asked Hare to the wood of the back door.

—The same that now was! came Lynch snapping back in way uncharacteristic of him. Moreover, his sequence of tenses was all off.

Hare didn't dare to answer straightaway. It was fearful to hear the laconic Lynch snap.

Lynch got up from the table. He came over to Hare at the door. Hare backed away. Lynch opened the door again. He looked out at the rain through the fissure, watching the striations on the slate sky.

Hare was trapped in a little enclosure made by the chair, the table and Lynch's body standing at the door. He waited.

After a moment Lynch turned round and looked hard at him.

—Supposing you get out of here, he said. When are you getting out of here?

—Soon, said Hare, the nape of his neck stiffening all on its own.

—Make it soon.

—I will make it soon, mumbled Hare.

—Make it soon. Do make it soon! Won't you make it soon! said Lynch, not going out of the kitchen, still looking and bringing forth his final phrase in a strange sing-song voice.

—You know what I told you, Hare, he went on.

—Of course, answered Hare gently.

—I told you, continued Lynch deliberately. I told you foot-finding time was limited.

—Of course, said Hare again, lamely. He had lowered his eyes out of humility. He could not miss seeing that Lynch's hand was shaking slightly in his cuff.

—I warned you.

Hare did not dare to answer because he knew it was Lynch's anger. He had never seen it before but here it was. And if it snapped who could tell in what direction it might spring? It had resolved itself, Lynch's eternal poise. For the first time it had gathered into another thing.

The hitherto ambiguous Lynch, irrecuperable, disparate and foliated, was in the dread process of revealing his doorway in. But Hare, on opening the door, realised it was the doorway out. There would be no clearer view of the Lynch edifice.

After the incident of the oxtail, things went from bad to worse. Lynch hid the supply of vodka, causing Hare to go scurrying round and round on his hands and knees looking in the cupboard under the sink and at the back of the various dwarfish pieces of furniture which lined the unfitted kitchen walls, until he found a bottle behind the fridge. He poured some out into his hip-flask and ran tap water into the vodka bottle.

Lynch took to putting the radio on loud in the kitchen as soon as he was up in the morning, which necessarily disturbed Hare from his pretend slumber. Needless to say, there was no more cup of tea on the bedside table, no more little attentions of any sort.

So that Hare said to himself: It'll serve him right. It'll serve him right if I get the vegetables from the supermarket instead of spending hours choosing what he likes from off the market stalls. Two can play at that game. It'll serve him right if the eggs are no longer fresh laid off the farm and the milk no longer fresh out of the cow. It'll all be just deserts to have him eating out of a tin regular, as no doubt he did before I turned up, poor muggins that I've been. Condensed milk instead of the real thing. Carrots out of a tin and his precious oranges and all.

So that the tin of oxtail, rather than spelling an exceptional occasion, came to be the beginning of the end as far as fresh country fare was concerned. Which served Lynch right, thought Hare, paring his nails over the kitchen table.

And as for trying to keep him cooped up here like a battery hen, thought Hare, we'll see about that. He pulled back the dirty white lace curtains of the sitting room and looked across the fields towards the steeple in which, it was said, Rosewall either hid or else surveyed the Battle of Tassin. A spot of city life would do him the world of good.

It seemed like an eternity since Hare had been back on his old stomping ground, the Opera quarter with the entire network of allies and brief strips of road that wound their way about it. He walked down Pizzay street and round the back of the building that housed the Opera Grill club. Then, realising he was coming up to his old hotel, he took a side street that led down towards the bank of the river. It was mid-afternoon and quite deserted. He walked slowly revelling in the stillness. The air was white. Snowflakes drifted across, but lone and abandoned, as if they had been chased from elsewhere. The street sloped down towards the river. The damp seemed to seep out from the flat cobblestones up through the soles of his shoes and so penetrate into his marrow.

He walked along the centre of the road, so sure was he that no vehicle would enter this precinct. Hare stood stock-still. He listened. The traffic droned in the distance. Two or three pigeons flapped a few yards from him. His own breathing rose and fell, rose and fell. He waited. He was halted as though in fog. The air stirred its silent coils about him. If now obliteration came, if now annihilation...

It was at this moment that Hare heard voices coming from a portico on the right. A man's voice and a woman's voice. Hare's first reaction was to look to hide himself in the next doorway, to extract himself from the broad daylight.

Even as he was hurrying across the cobblestones of the roadway he was thinking how ridiculous he was, for what reason on earth did he have for hiding from two anonymous individuals, one a man, the other a woman. He followed his body into the doorway. He stood there ignominiously, feeling as if the version of himself that he had always feared had finally gained the upper hand.

The man came out from the shadows of the portico. It was the Fox.

The Fox took leave of the woman. He kissed her on the mouth. The woman's back was to Hare, but he knew instinctively it was Dittmar's sister from the square of the shoulders. After a moment the Fox turned and made off in the direction of the river. His spouse watched him go off for a second before slipping back into the doorway.

Hare waited an instant before following her in. He heard her steps on the stairway. The door to an apartment opened and shut. The second floor. Hare looked at the list of occupants on the plaque by the letterboxes: Second Floor. Left. Vernon. Funny, thought Hare. Like the painter.

Hare trotted down the road after the Fox. He watched him turn onto the quayside. He chased his way along a back street that ran parallel to the quay. In this way he was able to head off the Fox and meet him on the pavement coming from the opposite direction.

—Good Afternoon! cried Hare on coming face to face with the brother-in-law.

The Fox looked at him for a moment, unable to quite conceive of the reality of the sudden apparition.

—Where did you come from? he muttered then, scarcely audible.

—Just taking the air, riposted Hare with all due offhandedness.

The Fox's suspicions were roused.

—You saw me coming out, he blurted after a moment.

—Yes, said Hare, smiling, as though this were the revelation of the mechanism of some gag.

The Fox wasn't smiling.

Hare was finding an area on himself to scratch, searching with his finger ends. The armpits, the ill-shaven chin, the nape of the neck.

—It's Dittmar's sister I saw you with?

—My wife, corrected the Fox.

—There never was a break-up between you two.

The Fox didn't answer. He gave Hare his quizative look.

—Come back to the apartment with me.

There seemed no reason not to. They walked back together. Isolated flakes of snow were still dashing across their path. Hare tucked his chin into his coat-collar. The air was chill. What a winter this had been! he thought. He almost said it out loud to the Fox, but thought better when he saw the stern expression on the face of the brother-in-law.

As they rounded the corner Hare caught a glimpse of the Dittmar poster.

—I see they've changed the poster, he said.

The Fox looked back at him with that unimpeded seriousness of his.

—What do you know about it? he snapped.

Hare winked at him.

—More than you think. More than you think.

Hare sniggered. It was true: he'd seen the redhead starkers.

The Fox is a dread enemy to mankind. Hare had read that somewhere recently, in some magazine. What they do is they urinate in the forest, on berries for example. Then Man comes along and eats the berries and ends up with this terrible disease, not rabies, but something like rabies. And if you ever get a look at the Fox's eyes, the article had said, then you'll know just what we mean.

They came in through the doorway of the block. Hare glanced at the name on the plaque once more. Vernon. Hare composed himself. Who was Vernon?

Was it possible that the painter Vernon lived here? Or maybe Rosewall. Why not Rosewall himself? Might it not be Rosewall behind the door whose bell Hare's guide, the Fox, was now ringing. Hare stood behind, aghast at the sudden and irreversible possibilities open to him. Then, suddenly remembering, he scratched at the shoulders of his coat to remove the possible dandruff.

The door opened an inch. The face of Dittmar's sister appeared at the gap. She unchained the latch.

—What is it?

—Let us in, said the Fox.

She was a little taller than her sister, surely a year or two older with the hint of a notch drawn above her nose where worry had been worn into her brow.

They were let into a bright and spacious room painted in white. The sister chained the door up behind them. There was a kind of acidic perfume he had smelt somewhere else in the air.

—It's Hare, said the Fox.

—Where did you find him?

—I happened to be in the quarter, interrupted Hare merrily.

They both looked at him.

—He was sniffing around outside, replied the Fox, putting the record straight.

—Now listen, started the sister, turning fully towards Hare. It's about time you told us what you're up to. You know what can happen if you don't.

Hare didn't really know. He stopped smiling though. That was the least he could do under the circumstances.

—Let's get one thing straight, he said, starting to move in the apartment, walking over to the table, looking at his own reflection in the mirror above the blocked-up chimney. You know something about Rosewall.

Even as he was saying this, concentrating primarily on his own reflection in the mirror, doing what he could to look the part, he noticed, out of the corner of his vision, another door in the reflection in the glass, and the thought, playful thought, drifted across his consciousness that Rosewall was perhaps behind that door. Why not? He had to be somewhere.

—Look! You're in no position to make demands, was the voice of the Fox. Where's the musket? he went on to the sister.

She went into what must have been the kitchen and came back with a musket that she handed over to the Fox. Hare had turned on his heels.

—This is a musket, said the Fox, fixing its muzzle on Hare at some point near the neck. If it shot and blew through his Adam's apple, that would be the end of it.

—Now tell me the truth. It's the time.

Hare realised that the moment had come to fix into words an invented truth.

—All right, he said. Just relax with that thing. I'm as good as gold.

He had put his arms in the air unbidden, as though he were an old hand in the business of musket threats.

—Just tell me what you're up to. That's all.

Hare could see the sister's resemblance to Dittmar clearly now. It was uncanny. The freckles of course. But also the line of the nose. The steepness of its fall from the brow. Pugnacious almost. A warrior's face.

—I'm investigating for the Agency, he told them.

—Go on, said the Fox and wiggled the point of his musket.

—Well, that's it. I'm supposed to write heraldry pieces and so what with the Rosewall arms scandal and that…It's obvious, isn't it? And then… No. In fact the truth is, I've dropped the Agency now. I've scarpered. I wrote that piece in The Herald. Did you see it? … No. Well, it wasn't exactly the kind of piece they wanted me to write. Still. A man's gotta write what a man's gotta write, if you get my meaning...Never mind. No. The point is now that it's personal, me and Rosewall. I was at school with him, see. He was a few years above me, but I remember him well enough. I just can't fit him in with as he is now, or was a short time ago... So, the point is, if Rosewall's here... I don't know, do I? He might be. He might be behind that door. He might be here, kept in security. Is that it?

—Why should he be behind that door? asked the sister.

—I don't know. But just say he was. He might be.

—Why would he be behind that door? was the Fox.

—He has to be somewhere.

—Who says he's somewhere? was the Fox again.

—But he might be, retorted Hare. Grant me that at least. He might be.

The sister glanced at the Fox. The Fox examined Hare.

—He might be, murmured the Fox at length.

—Can you put that gun down, said Hare, now that the subjunctive mood of Rosewall's existence was accepted.

The Fox motioned for Hare to sit down and placed the musket down on the coffee table. He laid his right hand beside it.

—Do you mind if I unbutton my coat? asked Hare.

The Fox acquiesced with a brief jerk of the head.

Hare unbuttoned.

—There is one question I'd like to ask you, he said as he fingered the buttons of his mac. Vernon.

The Fox's fingers moved back onto the musket.

—Vernon the Painter, said Hare. Does Vernon the Painter live here or what?

When Hare was mid-way through his sentence the thought struck him that if there was someone behind the door, it was Lynch. The cult of Vernon the Painter, the acidic perfume that was none other than Lynch's soap perfume. Hare was buttoning and unbuttoning the coat as he thought, as though his fingers were straying up and down the stops of a wind instrument.

—What do you know about Vernon the Painter? asked the sister, moving forward from the back of the room towards him. Hare noted the same heavy square of her shoulders as she stepped forward towards him. How would she look in an off-the-shoulder evening frock?

—Vernon the Painter, repeated Hare, feeling he had hit upon something. Ha-ha!

—Come back in three days, said the Fox.

—Why three days? asked Hare.

—Come back in three days, was the Fox again. And remember. We know who you are and how to get at you.

—Oh, I know that, said Hare buttoning up. I know that Rosewall could see to that if he wanted to. I'm sure that if Rosewall wanted to, he could do anything at all.

They saw him to the door and he went down alone.

PART FIVE

ENDING

SEVENTEEN

When Hare opened up the backdoor of the suburban house—he always came in round the back way—Lynch was out.

Hare sat down at the kitchen table and poured himself a vodka from his flask. He leaned across to switch the radio on. They were broadcasting news of different attacks. Unknown aggressors, they were calling them. Or so-called Phalangists. A bomb had blown off a woman's heel on Beaucourt Street. It was not sure whether or not the surgeons would save the leg. Others had perished immediately; the supermarket blast. A boy had lost an eye. Then news came through that a number of swarms of bees had escaped from a van transporting them to a trade fair in the North. The broadcaster was warning people to keep off the streets in the Opera quarter and near the Council Chamber.

Hare leaned back in his chair. He poured himself another vodka. Tonight was gala night. He wondered if the Phalange would dare an attack on the Opera House. That would make a fine gala if the Opera went up in smoke. Needless to say, Lynch would be there with his dolly birds. That slut Dittmar. He'd probably have a special box for the whole entourage. He'd be back soon.

He had to come back to get himself all dressed up. In the vicinity of the Opera House Lynch wouldn't be seen dead without his opera coat and those silk keks of his, especially gala night.

The rain was pattering. Hare looked out to it, following the paths of the tiny droplets that hurried down the windowpane to their respective oblivions.

When Lynch got back to the house he went straight upstairs. When he came down he was in his smoking jacket, white bow tie and fine silk trousers. In his hand he held his top hat. He smiled at Hare. A forthcoming kind of smile.

—There's half-an-hour to go, he said, looking at his wristwatch, before I leave. Just enough time for a little story. Let it be in the nature of a denouement for you. Tonight's gala night. It's also Winter Feasts' Cocktail Night for a few of us at the Opera Grill. When I return from the Grill, let it be that I no longer have you here. Let it be that you're no longer stirring in the corner of my eye, eh?

Hare shrugged. He looked at his pared nails. When he looked up Lynch was eyeing him. For Hare it was odd to imagine life, real life, in Lynch's skeletal body and in his eyes, now upon him, that were so sharp as to pick up on the briefest of gestures. It was true; Lynch was too spry to be human. The life in Lynch was not the life of your unextraordinary kith and kin. It was the next link in the chain after the sapiens, one step closer to the thinking, breathing skeleton: nimble, upright, aware (with antennae almost), able to flee from any danger and so continue its thinking, its breathing; adapting to all locations, inhabiting the light, the dark, transporting in its cased-up brain the dreams and useful myths of its previous lives, which sometimes at night in strange off-guard moments (who knows?) might haunt it.

—It's all over now, said Lynch. Tonight the Phalange will take control of the Council Chamber.

—You a Phalangist?

—You have said it, smiled Lynch. Have another drink. We tried to make a pact with Rosewall. A pact between Rosewall and the Phalange. It was the only way he could stay in power. What's the other word for it. A covenant. We tried to make a covenant. But Rosewall wasn't interested in a pact. The covenant was not to be.

Lynch got up from the table and went to the back of the fridge. He brought the vodka bottle out and poured Hare a glass. Hare knew how watered-down it was, but he said nothing.

When Lynch started to talk, twilight was happening all over, outside the house, in the suburbs and across the scrubland out to where the Rosewall steeple reached into the darkling sky.

—Picture the scene, he said. Cast your mind back. Recall those days. Rosewall's been gone from the city three days and three nights. It is known where he is. I'm talking about people in the know. They know where he is. In the Fourviere Forest with his band of men. He lives there. Don't ask me how he lives. Hunting the woodland creatures. Plucking berries from the trees. Poaching the chickens of the near-by farmyard. Lapping the water of the rushing brook. In any case, ravaging the plenty of the forest life. You know what I'm driving at.

Hare scoured the kitchen with his eyes. From time to time, when he passed across the talking mouth of Lynch, like a slim cloud across the waning moon, he saw a filling glint in his mouth. It would be a fabulous glimpse into the orifice, from whence the truth, all shimmering, or the lies, all shimmering too, were streaming forth.

—That's how he lived his life. I'm telling you what I know now. Outlawed in the Greenwood. There were rumours of it. But they weren't just rumours because I'm speaking to you now as a very organ of the rump Council Chamber. It was so. Go ahead! Pour yourself a vodka. Finish the bottle. It's the last one. Finish it off. Let's say it's my Winter Feasts' present to you. I'll stick to my milk, if you don't mind.

Lynch poured himself a glassful from the carton and sipped at it.

—And so it became clear that what was needed was for someone to go in there and chase him out of his hole and hunt him down and track him into a corner where there was no sheltering trunk and no twisty escape route and no backdoor and no way out of it and finish him off, him and his band of outlaws. And I was approached with a view to executing this job of work.

I've told you about my affiliation to the Council Chamber. I've told you about it. It's an odd affiliation in a way. A little kink in the hierarchy where you find me, off on a side-path. But it's true that certain jobs of work call for that little kink in the handing down of commissions which can let the package fall into my lap. And certain packages, once unwrapped, give certain jobs.

And so it comes to pass, if I may use such an expression, that I equip myself with a number of men...

—Warwick? interjected Hare.

—No, not Warwick, answered Lynch. But one fellow whose acquaintance you may have made. A Mr Gloucester. Gloucester the Engineer. He was numbered amongst my party. Trustworthy men. We clad ourselves in valour and we strode forth.

If you cast your mind back you'll remember it was summer. Difficult to imagine in the depths of this long winter which seems interminable. Remember how the sun beat down? We met together at five in the morning at the Opera Grill. It was before the daybreak. A number of vans were prepared. We got in the back. I remember how we slammed those doors shut. And then, when we got there, to the edge of the Fourviere Wood, where we were to pick up the dogs, we swung the doors open again, roughly, violently, on the rusty hinges…

Lynch smiled to recall the detail.

—Then we left the vans behind and went along the brow of the hill, skirting the forest. The city was below us. Day was infiltrating. The sky was heightening to a sombre blue. There was a haze on the river. You could just about see the dome of the Opera House above it, and the line of the old warehouses further up towards the Croix Rousse. We turned our backs to all this and advanced into the first thickets of the wood.

Lynch took a sip from his milk, his head tipping back on his shoulders to swallow it down like a bird.

—Have you heard about those wasps escaping from that lorry? he asked after a moment.

—I heard it on the radio, said Hare.

—You spend a lot of time with that radio on, don't you?

—It said they were bees.

—Wasps. Bees. What difference does it make? It'll keep people off the streets maybe. That's the main thing.

He paused, watching Hare closely and waiting for his response.

—Have another drink, said Lynch, pouring him one.

He began again, starting up slowly, methodically.

—I don't know if you can imagine it, Hare, but in the summer in the Fourviere Forest the green of it all takes you aback. There are places where the sun doesn't penetrate or just seems to come down like a heavy green tint, tinting everything, the men, the dogs, as if it were all taking place in an underwater kingdom or in some green dream. And that's what it is now anyway, a green dream.

Hare focused on a large jar of gherkins on the shelf.

—So if you're trying to imagine it, try and imagine it like that. In green. The baying hounds like strange fish

145

and the men hanging onto the leashes, panting hard behind in their leather breeches and cord trousers, a knife tucked in under the belt. Sometimes emerging into a clearing, the orange sun dappling them for a moment, before surging back into the heavy olive green liquid of the woods.

It was a three-litre jar of gherkins, three-quarters full of vinegar and half full of gherkins. The gherkins seemed suspended in the jar. Their surfaces were carbuncled, pustuled, cratered, pock-marked. They hung gracefully in the semi-opaque, slime-brown vinegar.

—Have you ever participated in a hunt, Hare?

—Never, answered Hare.

—I mean, of course, where you count amongst the hunters not the hunted, joked Lynch.

—No, never in a hunt.

—Well, I'm at a loss to describe the exhilaration of it all. The baying hounds, the tattoo of the footfalls on the cushioned forest track, the smell of the sweat, the antici- pation, the knowledge (sure and certain) that somewhere at the journey's end the hunted waits for us. And what would the hunted be doing at that moment? Smiling perhaps or whistling to himself, engaged in his moment, thinking he has all the time in the world to smile and whis- tle. And we, the green men, are bearing down on him, bearing down on that one particular tree where, today, for no special reason under the sun, he chose to sit himself down and snooze. The tree where we'll finally catch up with him and fork him. Perhaps just as he's finishing off his lunch and licking his lips clean of the chicken leg, before even the chicken has had the time to get down into the yards and yards of digestive tract, fork him.

The dark had fallen, silently, swiftly. Hare heard the rain slapping in the drainpipes, falling from gutter to gutter, clattering on the shed roof. On the grass it made no sound. The kitchen bulb was not switched on. Light came from the hallway and set itself down heavily in the kitchen in a block that just avoided the talking figure of Lynch. Hare saw how the speaker gently tipped and cradled the silhouette of his top hat to follow the lulls and cadences of his story.

—So, you'll be off to another little hotel when you finally clear out of here, will you? asked Lynch as he swallowed down some more milk.

—It could be, said Hare.

Lynch smiled.

—Tell me now, he said. What are you going to do? How are you going to live? Don't tell me. You'll follow in old Rosewall's footsteps. You'll pick up where he left off. Is that it? Cooking on an open fire. Sleeping under the stars. The night owl for music and the badgers for company.

Lynch laughed heavily from the lower lungs. It was as hearty a laughter as Hare had heard in him.

—Now you'll let me get on with my story, will you? I've embarked on this business. Now I intend to finish it. That way, I'll enjoy the gala night in peace. And in any case, I admit I'm almost pleased to be the one who lets you in on the secret. Not that it can be much of a secret to you by now, eh? You've raced ahead and guessed the end already, haven't you, you little rascal. But allow me to tell it through to the end in my own way. It will give me pleasure to, really it will. Now, where was I? Yes, the forest. Yes, the hunt. The baying hounds, the footfalls of the heavy men on the forest's ferny floor.

Though it's time I cut this long story short. So let me tell you this: we had knowledge of his exact whereabouts. He was hiding out in a woodsman's cottage buried deep in the heart of the forest. Picture it. We were pressing on. The sun was mounting higher in the sky. Dogs getting hungrier and hungrier. You see how it was. Though were it not for the aid of a humble forester who knew the woods like the back of his creased hand, we might well have passed by the thicket through which we were obliged to penetrate to gain access to the clearing in which the lonely cottage stood.

We came stealthily upon the hut, silencing the dogs as best we could. We approached on cat's feet. Up to the door. Our ears against the wood. Nothing. One of our number pushed it open with his foot. No-one inside. We went in. From what we could see of the belongings scattered haphazardly about the interior there were three of them. One of them was Rosewall. I examined the pack of documents that were surely his. The original drafting of the document that was later to become the Livestock Bill. Under his pillow a chain, some saint or other, Saint Anselm I think it was. And in a notebook, scribbled in his own scrawling and treacherously backward leaning hand, his projects for the razing to the ground of our schools and seats of learning. When I saw the notebook I was assured—as if I had ever really doubted—as to why we had come about our job of work. The papers, all of them, we burnt in a fire...

—And the medallion?

—The medallion, said Lynch. The medallion I do believe we confiscated.

And then we circled the hut and waited. We waited and we held our ears to the forest noises, and for men unaccustomed to the woods—men such as I—a forest wait for a forest bear like Rosewall is long indeed.

The gherkins had not stirred in their vinegar. They hung like charmed fish, ugly in their poor jar. They were under the spell of this or another story, or under no spell at all, just confounded, fish transformed to gherkins. In brief, gherkins.

—We waited, the treacle sun above, the forest about us, the air buzzing with insects. The dogs were resting, looking hard into space or into blades of grass without philosophy. The men—my men—resting too, though different in their rest, more restless than the dogs. And you know what I was thinking about? I said: do you know what I was thinking about?

—No, said Hare.

—I was thinking about Rosewall, and in particular, his crimes, his crimes against humanity. What Rosewall had done, his massacres.

There was a little pause.

—What massacres? queried Hare after the moment.

Lynch eyed him. Hare looked tangentially away. The gherkins had not moved.

—I am talking about massacres which are perhaps unknown to you. I am talking about massacres which I as an organ and member in all but name of the Council Chamber have access to and of which you are perhaps ignorant. I am talking of the monstrosities of the Four Month Rule swept under the mat. The hugger-mugger businesses of the Rosewall affair, which I had been entrusted to cast into the void once and for all, so that we might forget, better still never even know about his uneven handed justice.

Hare took a sip of his vodka. The rain was cascading along the gutters and splattering onto some stray slabs of concrete at the back of the house. Hare replaced his glass on the table and looked up. His eyes met Lynch's. They rested there for a moment. Lynch's eyes were dark grey.

—Listen to that rain, said Lynch.

They listened together.

—I tell you what. It'll do for those wasps, eh? What do you think?

Hare grunted.

—You know what's on at the gala tonight. It looks as if it's going to be quite a show. The line-up's really something. I'll bring you the programme back if you like. Oh no, of course not. I keep forgetting. You won't be here.

Never mind! Guess what! We've managed to get a box for the occasion. The whole gang's coming along. Well, it's a special occasion, isn't it? Winter Feasts' cocktail and all.

Now then. I mustn't digress. I must get this story finished double quick.

I'm casting my mind back. Back to that mid-summer's day. Try and picture yourself in there with us; that's the best way to understand.

Time stood still. Now I know that's fanciful, but there you are. Like it or lump it, time stood still. It was as if the universe was a universe of anticipation. All things flowed into that and it seemed impossible or unimaginable that the anticipation would at one moment reach its end. But it did.

The dogs sensed it first. They sat up. They pricked their ears. We knew it was the appointed time. They were coming back through the forest, strolling back. We heard them laugh together. Their last laugh. We waited. We held ourselves and the dogs still as long as it was possible. So that they would approach even closer to the hut. It became more and more difficult to restrain the dogs, their growls. There were ten dogs. We were fifteen men.

Until finally...until finally we let them run. We let them run and we yelped to encourage them. Picture yourself yelping with us, Hare. Yelping to encourage the dogs. We let out such mighty yelps as you never heard except in hell. And then we followed the dogs.

The threesome, Rosewall and his two lackeys, had fled on hearing the dogs. The first we tracked down some fifty or sixty metres off to the left. The dogs had dragged him down and mauled him. With the knives—didn't I tell you we had knives?—we finished for him. It's quickly done when ten men surround you. Or did I say fifteen?

Lynch took another sip of milk from his carton. A little spilt on his chin and trickled a moment before he wiped it off with the back of his hand.

—I've got to watch this milk. I don't want to go spoiling the eveningwear, do I? Anyway, the second was off to the right. The dogs got him too, pulled him down. We came hoofing after, quite comic it was, thinking it was Rosewall. When we got there, it wasn't. We did for him all the same. Left him there, not even hanging around to watch the fascinating blood come surging out. It was still flowing when we left him. We followed the dogs. Oh, it must have been a good five hundred metres through the undergrowth. Then, on coming on a clearing, we caught sight of him scrambling into the bushes on the left, the dogs just behind him. From that distance he was small. Of course, there was no reason to suppose he had become a large man suddenly. You know who I'm talking about, don't you?

Rosewall was running for his life. The blood had gone to my head too. My blade was strapped up against my hip. With the running I felt it scratching at my thigh.

Enough of the details. They serve no end.

A few moments later we came upon it, the untidy pile of the dogs and Rosewall squirming together. We watched it a moment, all of us. It was like a single beast engaged on some miraculous act; giving birth or in throes, one of the real acts. We were waiting till everybody had arrived. When the last of us had got there we went round and cleared the dogs away. Rosewall was on the ground looking at us. He was all mixed up with leaves and blood but you saw his eyes right enough. The whites were very white. You saw them right enough. He propped himself up on an elbow. I remember how he propped himself. As if his forearm was not a part of his body but a stick he used for propping himself. We were watching the business, somewhat surprised, surprised to find him there in a wood. Because after all, why be there and not elsewhere, like in a street or in a building some place? You know what I mean. It was Rosewall.

We waited. We hardly understood that the move was ours and not his. And right enough he made his move; propping himself up even further, onto his haunches, and then making efforts to get to his feet. We sensed we mustn't let him do such a thing. You can imagine.

It was Gloucester who stepped forward.

In trying to get to his feet Rosewall had somehow twisted, so that as he rose to his full height his back was turned. So, when Gloucester came forward with his knife it was the back of Rosewall he was confronted by. And when Rosewall turned round he was, I think, genuinely surprised to feel the knife going in. Just there!

And Lynch pointed to Hare, to a point somewhere. Hare followed the imaginary dotted line that led to his own abdomen. He bowed his head to it. The knife went in there then. At the point between the twin arcing of the rib cage, and then perhaps thrust up towards the heart.

—And that did for him! said Lynch. Let me hasten to add that although Rosewall was not quite facing his executioner at the moment of their first physical contact, the knife was nevertheless plunged into his front and not into his back. And Rosewall let out a great cry: Why did you abandon me? referring no doubt to his followers who had disappeared into thin air leaving him with just a couple of thieves who both lay bleeding dead one on either side of him. And he sank. Needless to say, we rushed forward to make sure of the job. Until he lay there still and it was Rosewall executed at our feet.

Hare, feeling the blow in his own body and blood, took his hands away from the place where the ribcage created a junction.

—And now it must be exit Lynch, said Lynch getting up. I'll be needing an umbrella, he said scouting round the kitchen. He found it; the black one, the gala night umbrella.

—And so it's goodbye Hare and adieu Hare and top luck Hare and then exit Hare too eh? Not forgetting always to give that door a good slam when you go and to leave the key on the kitchen table.

He went. Hare's eyes settled back on the gherkins. He rooted in his pocket for the nail file.

In the empty house, Hare turned his gaze onto the furniture. He thought of what Lynch had said. How had he put it? The all-conquering inanimate, he had said, speaking about the furniture in Vernon's paintings.

There was one armchair in particular. It was large as though it might have been made for a person of unusual bulk. Lynch had never reupholstered it nor recovered it. Hare had the impression that Lynch had never even thought of recovering or reupholstering it, that the thought had never crossed his mind for an instant. It was just sedately going its way to wrack and ruin, the armchair. In the perfectly silent house it stood, its arms outstretched to confine and protect its archetypal sitter of bulk. When you looked at the armchair in its profile, its arms outstretched in that unchanging gesture, it was difficult not to think of the gesture as significant, as prayer or service. The fixed functions of the inanimate were so many small, heathen prayers.

Hare thought of his own death. What small prayer might he address and where might he direct it? The chair worshipped its archetypal man of bulk. To what archetypal bulk might Hare deliver himself?

EIGHTEEN

When Hare arrived at the sister's building in the little road that ran down to the river, he looked up to the windows on the second floor as if he might see the silhouette of Rosewall framed there, the unholy fall of the shoulders, the too perfect oval of the head, the elevation of the bust surging up from below the level of the window-sill. There was no such form visible at the window.

—I have to see Rosewall, he said when the door was open to him.

—Three days you were told, said the sister.

—Let me see him now. It's important. There's no time to wait three days.

—Who says he's here? she said, letting him in.

The door to the backroom was open. Hare marched across to it and into the neighbouring room. A single bed was in the corner, perfectly made with crisp white sheets. It was as slim a single bed as Hare had seen. Beside it a bedside table with a lamp. There was an armchair and a commode by the window.

—I don't know where he is, said Hare as he inspected the empty room. But he might be. There again he might not be. He might be dead. Assassinated. Hunted like an animal. That might be true, too. What do you think?

The redhead's sister was saying nothing. She was over by the door to the empty room holding the lintel with one hand, a ring on her finger, her hip abutting.

—A single bed, eh? said Hare. What do you get up to in that? I mean: you live here alone, do you?

She narrowed her eyes.

—I need to be taken to Rosewall if he's alive.

She still didn't answer.

—Be he alive or be he dead, said Hare, going over to the window.

—If you think he's dead why do you need my assurance?

—I don't believe Rosewall can be dead.

—You think he's immortal, do you?

—I don't think he's dead. You're telling me he isn't dead, more or less. Everything you do, everything you say tells me he isn't dead. The way you ask me your questions, the way you hedge in your answers, or even the way you move or flick your hair back...

The conquest of the two sisters would be quite something. It would be as if he was coming home from the hunt with a pair of partridges slung over his back. It wouldn't hinder him picking up the pelt of a certain Rosewall either.

The sister had turned and walked back into the main room. Hare followed.

—You know I know your sister, said Hare to the back of the striding woman.

—Do you? she said, not bothering to turn. She was at the table of the main room.

—We had a bit of a thing, said Hare, nodding his head, his bottom lip flapped over the upper, a smile visible perhaps only in the dimples that had suddenly appeared in his cheeks.

—It's all over now, he went on to explain. You know what it's like sometimes.

The sister had worked her brow into furrows. She was taking a cigarette out from a packet on the table. She eased it out from below and flicked it into the flat of her hand, before picking it up and placing its end into her lips. She looked at Hare, her green eyes half-closed in their orbits.

—Why aren't you at the gala night? asked Hare. They could do with some fancy tart like you to smarten up the proceedings. This is when it's all happening, right?

—This is when it's all happening, she echoed disdainfully. You can see there's no Mr Rosewall here. Why don't you piss off?

Hare watched her fingers working together to get her match lit. Then, when the cigarette was in action, the smoke was trickling across her left eye.

—Think you're pretty cool, don't you? said Hare.

She didn't stir.

—You know I could twist your arm up your back and get the information I want out of you that way, or flick your ears for you. How would that be?

He watched her. Her nostrils dilated deliciously. He could and all. She was wearing a yellow dress.

—I said how would that be? he repeated, not taking his discourse any further, just watching her.

—What do you want from me? she said.

—Information.

—You don't want information from me. You want something else.

—What?

—You want something else. You want to get me up against that wall.

—Why?

—To put your hands on me. To rip off my canary dress and put yourself up against me. That's what you want.

—Don't worry! I already sampled your sister.

The heavy bronze bracelet she was wearing round her arm had fallen down onto her wrist.

She pulled the amulet back into position. The monstrous curl of contempt on her upper lip was too much to bear.

—I already sampled your sister, repeated Hare.

His face had turned red as he advanced towards the sister. She was staring at him. They were about the same height. Hare brought his arms out of inaction and pinned her against the wall, pressing her forearms against the white wall. Hare pushed his pelvis up against her. She tried pushing him back but she couldn't. Hare felt his face freezing into place as he leaned forward to hold himself heavily against her. She said some words but they were coming from another part of her throat now and Hare didn't make out what she was talking about because of the blood rushing in his ears.

From there he managed to turn her down onto the floor. She was writhing in his grasp. He managed to pull down the front of her dress a little way and reveal her frontage a little more. At this moment, just as he was turning his attention to the lower hem of her dress and scratching it up to reveal her black knickerwear, he felt her struggling pelvis push into him and the whole operation exploded, silently, undramatically, hopelessly. Too much time spent alone. Too little on-site activity. She freed an arm and her elbow caught him on the cheekbone. The blow brought a word out of him:

—Information, he said.

She threw him off and scrambled to her feet. Hare got up and moved over to the door.

—All right, all right, he said. I already sampled your sister in any case.

He fumbled at the lock of the door.

—Scram! she said as he was opening the door, and he just had the time to say huh! before the door slammed shut behind him.

Hare took a hotel room at the top end of the street. He tucked himself up in bed early and put the alarm on for seven in the morning. By half past seven he was out on the street looking up at the sister's silhouetteless window. When he had stowed himself away in a doorway opposite for the wait, he looked down at his unpolished shoes in which he had trekked so far. It might be, he told himself, that one final trek would take him to Rosewall, his actual skeleton, cadaveric or quick. With the ball of a finger he rubbed the vein-webbed ball of the eye through the lid. His eyes were red.

The tarty bitch, he said, thinking of the tight fit of the sister's yellow dress around the bust and hips. He would have got her up against the wall too. Just to hammer some quiet into her. He'd get the information out of her that way. He'd get more than information out of her. He'd have her slavering it out, the information. Talk of information, it'd be pouring off her by the time he'd finished with her. He'd leave her more than moistened up after the outflow of information. She'd be left trembling on that narrow bed, the yellow of that yellow canary dress all changed to a different yellow with the moisture on her after his extraction of her information.

At ten o'clock she appeared on the pavement below and walked swiftly towards the centre of the city. Hare followed at a distance. She turned down the Jacobins Street heading towards Charity Street and the Railway Stockyards. Jacobins Street turned slightly in its long unferlment as though it were the fraction of an immense arc that might girdle the city. The sun was out.

She went directly past Haberdasher's Yard continuing her way towards the Railway Yards and the old warehouses of the quarter, which had been undergoing a massive renovation programme before the troubles started.

When she arrived at the point on the road where all the traffic veered off, she turned away to the right into a narrow passage which led by the back of an old warehouse. The scent of cinnamon hung in the air. Hare waited and let her advance. After a moment he went after her.

At the end of the passageway the path issued out onto a worksite. The sister was on the far left of the plain—for it was a plain—picking her way over the bricks and heaps of concrete towards the long line of another warehouse. When she had slipped between the edge of the warehouse and a workman's hut Hare began to cross the plain himself.

It was the beginnings of a housing estate. Prefabricated walls were piled up on each other like giant packs of cards. Over towards the left some other houses had been elevated but were waiting facadeless, on the inside uncompleted staircases winding nowhere. Hare stepped over the fragment of a concrete staircase lay on its side on the ground. The entire site gave more the impression of being the remains of an antique city with its debris and trunkless pillars than the elements of a modern community.

When Hare arrived by the workman's hut, the Fox was waiting for him with his revolver pointed. His wife was at his shoulder. Together they made a family portrait: Fox and Spouse.

—I knew you were following me from Charity Street, she said, brushing her hair back over her forehead with a movement of her hand, the precise attentions of the forefinger gathering up all the strands of her fringe into a bundle that she dropped behind her ear.

—What's your game? said the Fox.

—I'm looking for a man, said Hare.

The Fox and his wife ignored him.

—How's Vernon? she asked.

—Vernon's fine, said the Fox.

Hare looked from one to the other, but they were both looking into space.

A man emerged from behind a wall twenty yards back. He asked what was up. Nobody answered. He came over. The Fox screwed up his face and his glasses slipped down his nose a little way.

—Take my glasses off, he said to his wife.

She did so, folding the arms and putting them into her overcoat pocket.

—It's Hare, she said to the other man.

—We can't keep him here, said the man. He was wearing a chain round his neck with a silver badger on the end. When the party turned off together to make their way to the doorway of an old warehouse that lay at the back of the wall, Hare noticed the keys jangling about on the man's waistband, such large ungodly keys, whole barrels of metal.

They took the fire stairs that were on the exterior of the building up to the second of the three floors and pushed open the wooden door. They came into a small room with two tiny square windows. Light fell in dull patches onto the dusty matted floor.

—Shut up and sit down, said the Fox and gave the gun to the other man, who took hold of it somewhat reluctantly as though it were some creature abhorrent to him. The Fox went through into another room.

Hare did not think to open his mouth. He glanced at the man with the crucifix who was watching him slowly as if he were likely to make a slick move. The sister was waiting stiffly on one leg, searching in her handbag for something. After a moment she came out with her lipstick. She turned her back on Hare to put it on, looking in her compact mirror.

—I don't know why you smear that jam all over your mouth, said Hare.

The man with the crucifix looked concerned. The sister didn't answer. She snapped her handbag shut.

Somewhere Hare could hear the sound of a saw to-ing and fro-ing through a piece of wood. Hare listened closely to it. There was comfort in the idea that the job was finding its completion by following the simple mechanics of the instrument. It was a reassuring sound. There was no jarring. It didn't let up. It was the cradle that rocked Hare deeper.

Behind the sawing another sound persisted. It was a kind of distant babel, the endless drum-roll of human voices living in the furthest of audible backgrounds. As Hare strained his ears to listen, the picture formed in his mind of the warehouse as a hive with each of the many partitioned-off rooms containing a separate human enterprise. The room above, the room below, to the left, to the right: each held its own intimate dramaturgy, its own protagonists, its own agonists. Hare looked down to his mud-soiled shoes. The he shifted his gaze onto the zip on his trousers, making sure it was up.

While his head was bowed a door swung open. A figure had strode in. Hare looked up. Standing before him was Gloucester. Hare wondered if it would be right for him to smile or to say *now we're getting places.*

—Hare, said Gloucester, moving forwards.

Hare had never actually spoken to Gloucester before. He felt a thrill of excitement that he should be recognised. Perhaps they all spoke about him when he wasn't there. He had never really examined Gloucester's face before either. It was brow-dominated, doom-laden, like a huge ant head. He was inspecting Hare. Hare stood up. He was searching for a clue in Gloucester's eyes. It was he who had been the executioner. Gloucester the Engineer. Gloucester the Executioner. Gloucester the Salamander. It was he who had dealt the final blow in Lynch's ballad of the hunted Rosewall.

Hare opened his mouth to pose a question but before he could speak Gloucester said: Come with me.

Hare emitted a kind of short sigh.

—Where are we going? he said.

And Gloucester answered as though it were in the nature of things: To see Rosewall.

NINETEEN

Rosewall's face existed in Hare's consciousness like the impression of the prophet's face on the shroud. Its broad lines were etched on the plate of his brain like the photocopy of a mediocre photograph. Its two or three shades of black and grey gave him the rough lines of the jaw and cheeks and the shading of the eyes, the hair fit on like a close dark skull cap.

As he was escorted through the endless corridors and rooms of the hive, he tried to work the print-out representation into the snag of some reality, but the head refused to take on human proportions. When he sat down to wait in what could only be the final vestibule of this our story and swallowed his final spittle, watching a final door, waiting for a final opening and a final revelation, he searched in vain for a sense of finality in his own head. He looked down to the zip on his trousers. He checked it was up. He scratched the possible dandruff from the shoulders of his jacket. What other preparations could there be? He could see the vertical of another dullness issuing from the inch-wide shaft between the door and its frame. A steel-grey dullness as of ash. There was no possible preparation.

The door swung back and Gloucester, his eyebrows veering down and in towards the top of his nose, beckoned with his hand. Hare stepped forward and advanced towards the grey light.

It would be wrong to talk of the moments that followed in the bated breath that one links up to salvation or epiphany or communion or annunciation—any of these things. It would be smarter to say that reality, which had been inching along after its own fashion, finally got that last little nudge that fitted it into place. The whole business that had gone before comes out looking like the subterfuge and fiction of this moment, an evil horseplay serving just to frame or highlight. But then, as we say, that's not strictly the case. It's just the moment when Hare meets Rosewall.

And coming forward, prompted by someone (Gloucester), to the bench against the wall where the presence (Rosewall) was. It was him. There was no doubt about it. The plane of the forehead, the shading of the jaw, the grain of the skin all spoke out affirmations. Hare experienced a pleasant little shock to his digestive system. He came opposite Rosewall, the banal-looking man, and was drawn in by the play of the brows and eyes which is enough to convince Hare that it is like this: that Hare is drawn out from his rib as Woman was from Man.

In what must have been the manifestation of that vocation, Hare thrust his hand down his pants and hooked his dick out from the left partition of his underpants and into the right with the crook of his finger. Penis dexter.

Rosewall was a large man with heavy, important, earnest features: a nose leaning somewhat to one side like the helm of some wayward steering vessel, his eyes underscored by pads delineated by creases, the hair pulled round the back of the ears and curling back round below them, needing to be cut, giving him that life-involved air.

The neck was ruddied from the protracted business of blading down with a razor. The flesh had pimpled up there in reaction. The line of the jaw was long and clean, but at the chin the cheeks hung heavy like the pockets on old trousers, making useless scabbards for the warrior. Rosewall was budging himself this way and that. He was shifting his nervousness, tugging it here and there. He'd come to terms with his features: hands (hair sprouting on the lower joints of the fingers); the narrow propped pod of his shoulders with the brazen rugged head fitted above it; the set of his mouth, cloven straight across the banged fruit of the head above the fine chin draped by the cheek scabbards.

Rosewall was, as everyone knew, a middle-aged man. That is to say in this particular case that the elements of youth and old age both courted the face, the former having drunk deep and appearing from behind a gauze as though it were retiring into nothingness, and the latter existing in the bud, as a glimmer, an unseen courtier promising his services from the shadows of Rosewall's inner chamber.

Hare. Finally to come to terms with the short-arse. His inner chamber, which had always resembled a Bluebeard's Castle with its multitude of secret doors and phoney ins and outs. But mainly, he had always kept his backdoor open. He knew the whereabouts of the trap-door and the fire-door, the tradesman's exit and the servant's stairs, the secret passage behind the bookcase and the one behind the fireplace, not to mention the uses of the two-way mirror and the garden maze, nor, for that matter, the elegant sash windows, where one need simply cock a leg to nip out and escape the reckoning. Of course, houses-capes were the terrain of any man, but he, Hare, was—was he not, gentlemen of the jury?—particularly adept in all those fancy gettaways and hideaways. It had got so as he could hardly cross the ill-lit corridor of an idea without one of his slanting eyes calling forward the white light beyond the sash windows.

All this now: stopped, ended! The face of Rosewall. An undramatic face. Perhaps the face of the brother he never had. A face you would be hard put to peel from the neutral or conventional. A face. Just a face. Let it rest there! After all the shuffling of hither and thither. Let this face, or these faces, be an end to it. To say, let it end, is almost in the manner of a prayer. Does it matter that we define it or that Hare defines it? Let it end soon. That is all. Let it end soon.

These were the many faces that Hare saw: the warrior's, the politician's, the old man's, the unswashbuckling and ordinary face, the simple etch of he who was on the bank note, the face of genius with its concentration of interests immediate and remote behind the eyes, a dusty and unremarkable face, a face with the ability to wrest light from others, a face of smothered light, light sacrificed to direr necessity. And then there was also the face Hare loved, for Hare has always loved Rosewall. And each version of his face was adumbrated upon the other to form the meaninglessness of the texture that let its shadow fall upon Hare as he entered the room. Hare prepared to wed himself to that texture.

Except this one thing, which is merely a detail.

TWENTY

—There's your Rosewall for you, said Gloucester and hurried Hare back out of the room.

He was taken into another room and confronted by Lynch.

—Sit down Hare, said Lynch.

Hare sat down facing a large rough etching of the projected Gloucester coat-of-arms which was pinned to the wall.

Lynch was speaking:

—Tomorrow the final Vernon poster will go up. The final Vernon poster which is the sign all the Phalange cells are waiting for to spring into action. The Council Chamber has already been infiltrated. The whole mechanism leaps into action tomorrow. The Phalange takes power. Password Vernon. Rosewall is given the public execution he warrants for his crimes against humanity. The city finds its face once more.

Hare made to speak, but could not. The weight of these last few weeks lay upon him. He felt heavy. His eyelids were heavy, his tongue heavy, his legs heavy, his head heavy on his neck. But it was all O.K., he felt. Now he knew what existed and what did not. Vernon tomorrow, his fictitious brother not, Prospect hardly, Dittmar not mattering, Lynch and Gloucester arm in arm, Rose-wall yes, still existing but only just. It was a case of lies vanquished, reality unveiled.

Hare had half-turned towards Gloucester in the way the fictional Rosewall had turned in the famous ballad of the Hunt of Rosewall. Hare (short-arse, eternal third party, dupe, scapegoat, figure of fun, buffoon, elaborate fake, dweller in life's suburbs and only child) listened as Gloucester was saying something.

Hare was genuinely interested but behind him he could already hear the revolver being adjusted in the execu-tioner's hand and his dry palm opening up to grasp it comfortably. Hare looked across towards the red cray-oned eyes of the reptile salamander and prepared for the other, nastier ending.

The Knot Garden

—And so, Hare. You are walking now. Your feet take you easily over the terrain. Your legs are no longer heavy. You are walking. Where are you walking?

—I am walking through a forest. Though the trees are falling away. It is no longer a forest now. It is a garden.

—What kind of a garden?

—An ornamental garden. It is actually, unless I am very much mistaken, a knot garden.

—A knot garden. Do you stop to admire the plants and designs of this knot garden or are you hurrying on to get somewhere?

—I am admiring the dwarf hedges in the shape of interlacing ribbons. From each planting bed I smell the perfumes of a bouquet of herbs.

—Tell me, which species of herbs do you smell?

—Marjoram and thyme. Lemmonbalm and camomile. Rosemary, marigolds, pansies, spring violet.

—Splendid. But how is this wealth of sensular delight arranged?

—In geometric forms. Each small bed separated from the next by a narrow pathway.

—What geometric forms?

—Brick circles, diamond parallels, interlocking diamonds. Now I am passing an oval parterre of spring violets.

—You seem to know a lot about the knot garden. Pray, how did you come by such erudition.

—Unclear.

—Do you linger by the spring violets.

—No. I am hurrying on.

—Why are you hurrying?

—I want to get into the house.

—The house? So there is a house?

—Yes. At the end of the knot garden.

—Describe the house.

—It is three floors high and many rooms across. It is highly elaborate.

—What colour is it?

—A rich burgundy-coloured stone house with an elaborate roof onto which I could perhaps climb.

—Is that your aim?

—Yes. It is my first aim.

—Why is this?

—I would like to see the surrounding countryside from a vantage point.

—But the house is only three storeys high.

—High enough in such a flat landscape.

—So where do you go now?

—To the front door.

—You forsake the knot garden.

—The knot garden is behind me now.

—You do not think to turn back and enjoy the sweet scents of, say, the lavender maze.

—No, I advance to the front door.

—So be it. The front door then. Is it open?

—It opens to my touch.

—Describe the house.

—It is a fine residence. I am in a large atrium. There is a staircase ahead of me.

—Do you advance towards the staircase or do you prefer to explore the possiblilities on the ground floor.

—I go upstairs.

—The ground floor holds no charms for you.

—It does not. My eyes are focused on the banister that leads upstairs.

—Are the stairs in any way remarkable?

—There are paintings on the wall as I go up.

—What kind of paintings? The usual collection of ancestors and great-great-grandfathers?

—Perhaps. I don't know. I only have eyes for one painting.

—What is this painting?

—It is the picture of a painter painting on his canvas.

—What is his subject?

—A group of characters.

—Do you know any of these characters?

—Yes. They are figures from my life.

—Can you name any of these figures?

—I cannot, but they are familiar to me.

—Is there anything else on the canvas worthy of comment?

—The painter is working on a particular figure at the moment. This figure is of particular interest to me.

—For what reason is this figure of particular interest to you?

—The figure is perhaps me.

—Why only perhaps? Can you not recognise your own features?

—I am unable to. My own features are no longer clear to me.

—Can this be true?

—It must be. There is as you speak a mirror by which I am passing, but as I go to focus on my image I lose concentration and in a moment the mirror is passed.

—Is there not perhaps another reason why you are unable to see your own features in the painting?

—What do you mean?

—Is there not perhaps another reason why you are unable to recognise your own features in the painting?

Look at the painting once more. Look at your head and body in the painting. What is the painter doing?

—My head and body are indistinct.

—What is the painter doing?

—He is effacing my features.

—Has he changed his mind about painting you in?

—Unclear.

—Has he no longer any need for you in his scene?

—Unclear.

—But you are effaced. So much is clear.

—Yes.

—And now you are moving on. You are continuing on up the staircase. You arrive at the top of the staircase. Where are you now suddenly?

—I am on the roof.

—What kind of a roof is this?

—Flat. With many chiminies.

—Do you look out across the countryside? Does it lay before you as a chessboard?

—It does.

—What do you see?

—I see the runnels of brooks and meadows. There are many creatures down below. Some benign. Others less so. Butterflies and foxes.

—It is a land you will explore another day.

—No. It is all inaccessible to me now. I will never set foot on that land again. The foxes and the butterflies will continue without me.

—Where do you go next?

—I go back down into the house. I breathe the fresh air for the last time. Now I need to close my eyes.

—You are back on the stairs now. What do you see?

—I see an opened door into a bedroom.

—Do you see the bed?

—Yes.

—What kind of a bed is it?

—High. A high bed.

—Do you go into the bedroom?

—I go into the bedroom.

—Do you close the door after you?

—I close the door after me.

—Is the bedroom empty?

—The bedroom is empty.

—What do you do?

—I climb into the bed.

—With your clothes on?

—I do not get undressed. I just climb into the bed.

—What kind of a bed is it?

—I have told you. A high bed. It is of no matter. I am drowsy.

—But you take your shoes off at least?

—Unclear. I am drowsy. I pull the heavy counterpane over my head.

—But you won't be able to breathe.

—Unclear. I heap the counterpane onto my body. It covers me up.

—But you don't even know whose bed this is.

—It is my bed. The bed is ready for me to sleep in. The counterpane obliterates me now. I am asleep. It is not sure whether I am even still in the bed. I have shrunk beneath the counterpane. The impression of a body has gone. The body has been taken into the bed. It is finished.